SHARKWATER BEACH

TIM MEYER

SEVERED PRESS
HOBART TASMANIA

SHARKWATER BEACH

For my wife, Ashley.
My lighthouse in the dark, treacherous seas of life.

TWO DAYS AGO

It had been a normal day at the office until a small, bleating red dot on the computer monitor shook Teddy McDermott free from his daydream. He put down the cupcake his wife had baked him the day before and wiped the fallen sprinkles off his white polo T-shirt. A green smudge near the company logo remained the only evidence he had been snacking and daydreaming instead of working. "Shit," he muttered, licking his fingers. He tried to rub out the stain with his thumb but to no avail. His saliva only made the blot blurry and wet.

Abandoning his effort to erase his sloppy mishap, Teddy cursed himself for being such a scatterbrain. If he had paid more attention to his job, he might have avoided the incident altogether. But instead of dealing with computer's blinking red nuisance, he was thinking of how to explain the recent mysterious text messages he'd been receiving to his wife, Sara. And he would need to explain because the woman had the uncanny ability to *know* things, to see into his head. It was as if every secret he ever owned had been printed on his forehead and she was the only one who could read them. She was the twenty-first century female version of Sherlock fucking Holmes.

Maybe that was wrong. Maybe she wasn't extraordinary. Maybe *he* was the problem. Maybe his guilt was as obvious as the gap between his front teeth.

Whatever the case, Teddy couldn't think about it any longer. The bleep on the screen grew louder and faster, and he had work to do. He leaned in and examined the monitor. The red dot flared, faded, then flared again. The map next to his computer told him this particular "event" was taking place inside Sector 7, near the isolated containment chambers. This was a curious place to have a security breach because as far as Teddy knew, Sector 7 had been a dead zone for years. At least since he'd been hired.

Nothing should be near those containment chambers, he thought as he picked up the radio and adjusted the knob, turning on the appropriate channel.

Before Teddy could say his name, Pierre said, *"Yes?"* as if this were the hundredth time Teddy had called him that afternoon. In actuality, this was only the second occurrence.

"Sorry to bother you, boss," Teddy replied.

Silence on Pierre's end—the long kind.

"Pierre? You there?"

No answer.

Teddy didn't care much for his boss, and he wasn't alone. The other security guards talked shit behind Pierre's back, called him names Teddy found worthy of busting a gut. If it were anyone else, Teddy might not have found the childish monikers funny. But because Pierre was a total dick to him, he figured it was okay to have a laugh at his expense. He walked around the place like his piss smelled like Armani cologne and he shit rainbow sherbet. Granted, he did look like Jean-Claude Van Damme, acted like him too. Word in the hallways was Pierre got laid a lot because of this. Whatever. Teddy didn't look like Jean-Claude Van Damme. Teddy looked like Chris Farley, post *Beverly Hills Ninja* years.

Almost every time they spoke, Pierre and Teddy clashed, so Teddy spent the better part of his day avoiding his boss. He only called him when something above his security clearance was required. Unfortunately, those situations came up frequently. Luckily today had been quiet. Only one issue prior to the breach in Sector 7.

"Pierre? Can you hear me?"

Static on the other end, then, "Yeah, I hear you. Dammit." Teddy visualized his boss's face melting with anger.

"Do you need me down there?" He checked his watch. "I could be down there in five—maybe ten minutes." He looked up as if he'd forgotten something. "Unless the elevator is on the fritz again—"

"No," Pierre responded. The brevity of his response somewhat surprised Teddy. "Stay put. Call you if I need you."

That was a kind way of saying, *Fuck off, you insolent moron.*

Static conquered the radio and soon after, Pierre was gone, leaving nothing behind but silence.

"Good riddance," Teddy said, leaning back in his seat. It wasn't long before he closed his eyes and returned to his predicament: Sara and the situation at home. If she hadn't snooped around his text messages yet, she was bound to. He'd spent the last week living in fear, thinking one day he'd come home to find her in the kitchen, waiting with printouts of his message history, eager to sift through them and listen to his explanation, for which he hadn't one yet. He imagined the finger-pointing and the yelling that would follow those awkward moments. If he was lucky, he'd manage to walk away without getting an open palm across his face.

Not that he didn't deserve one.

Fact was, he had grown tired of Sara. Bored. Between their two jobs, they hardly saw each other. Whenever he brought the work thing up she suggested they have a baby. Her claim was that creating another life would bring them closer together, back to a time when things were all sunshine and rainbows and perfect. Teddy didn't want kids, wanted nothing to do with responsibility of that magnitude. Plus, kids were annoying and smelled funny. And they'd impede his freedom. He wanted to be available when his buddies asked him to hang out after work, head to Hooters for burgers and beer. Not forced to come home to a wife and screaming baby. She didn't want to hear any of that, though. Sara swore she'd coerce him into making babies down the road, even though they were thirty-three and there wasn't much road left.

Bullshit, she had said. *People have babies into their forties and fifties nowadays.*

Oh boy. Another argument she couldn't put down.

In what could be considered a dick move, Teddy didn't want to leave Sara outright. He had thought about it on several occasions, nearly every other day at this point, and he couldn't bring himself to do it. For one, his parents were a zealous Christian bunch and divorce was as evil as rape and murder in their eyes. He couldn't initiate the process. Nope. It had to come from her end. He had to get creative.

So, he met a girl. *Katie.* The new marine biologist on Sub-Level 3. She was sweet. Cute. Glasses. Long hair pinned back to make it look shorter than it was. A real bookworm. They'd started talking when he caught her reading the new Hunter Shea novel in the break room. That sparked a twenty-minute conversation on books, monsters, and their favorite 80s horror icons. They discussed their favorite novels and authors. Katie confessed her all-time favorite scribe was Peter Benchley, which made a lot of sense the more he thought about it, her being a marine biologist and all. He said he enjoyed the novel *White Shark*. She went on to tell him how that was her idol's weakest effort and that *Jaws* was the pinnacle of Peter Benchley novels. He admitted to having never read it and she laughed, chided him playfully and laughed some more.

And, well, that's how it started. And from there it never really stopped.

Katie texted him all day, every day. So much that he sometimes couldn't keep up with replies. Day, night, home, work—didn't matter. It got so bad he had to turn his phone off at home to keep Sara's suspicions at bay. He had to excuse himself to the bathroom so he could turn it back on and answer all her messages. He'd taken a lot of "shits" at home over the last few weeks.

He didn't know why he hid it from her. Fear, he figured. Sure, he wanted things over with Sara, was beyond ready for his new life to begin, but something held him back. Maybe it was because they had spent the last fifteen years together and throwing away all that history wasn't the easiest thing to do. Plus, who was to say things would work out with Katie? Sure, things were great *now*. But they hadn't even hung out together outside the S.Q.U.I.D, the subaquatic research facility they both worked at. Their relationship had never dipped outside of the *friend zone*, although he pictured things taking a romantic turn once he ditched the weight on his ring finger. He sensed they shared a mutual attraction.

Katie's face disappeared from his thoughts when the dot on the computer monitor bleeped again. Louder this time, as if the noise were originating from the center of his brain. He reached for the button marked "silence" but not before another siren screamed in his ear, this one alerting him of an event in Sector 6. Then something triggered the alarms in Sector 4. The three alarms screeching simultaneously lanced his eardrums.

What the hell is happening down there? wondered Teddy.

He picked up the radio and switched to Pierre's personal frequency. "Pierre? You copy? Pierre, we got alarms going off all over the damn place. Everything all right down there?"

No answer.

"Pierre? Do you need my assistance?"

Static remained the only response.

"Last chance before I come down th—"

Through the interference, he heard intermittent screams. Short bursts of terror. Men and women crying for help, screaming as if unexpectedly faced with their final moments. And...

Water?

Teddy couldn't tell if that was background static or turbulent waves crashing.

He jumped from his seat like someone lit a match in the crack of his ass. He wiped a stack of unnecessary paperwork off his desk with his arm, hands scrambling around until they landed on his keys. Jamming them into his pocket, he grabbed the radio. He cranked the volume up to *MAX*. It played mostly static now, but every ten seconds or so he heard someone call out for help, followed by a bloodcurdling scream.

Teddy rushed out of his office and headed for the stairs. He barreled through the stairwell door and stamped down the steps two at a time. The action left him breathless. Back in high school, he could have jumped down the entire flight in one bound and still been able to carry on without feeling like his heart would explode, but not anymore. Now he carried around a beer gut, which hampered his athletic ability. He hadn't seen his toes in almost ten years. It probably didn't help to have a fried chicken joint at the end of his block, but that was trivial now. When he reached the bottom of the stairs he bent over and placed his hands on knees, waited for his breath to catch.

Once the invisible elephant jumped off his chest, he left the stairwell and entered the S.Q.U.I.D's main level.

The S.Q.U.I.D—a complicated acronym that Teddy learned five years ago but had long since forgotten—was a subaquatic research facility located roughly 200 nautical miles off the coast of Florida, somewhere in the Gulf between the United States and Mexico. Privately owned and operated in non-territorial waters, few people—except for employees and a few government officials on the take—knew of its existence. Teddy knew whatever went on here, whatever "research" was happening, wasn't sanctioned by any legit organization, and if it were, whoever funded the projects didn't want anyone to know about them. Teddy's paychecks were signed by Karl Petruski III, and the name of the company on the top left was "Petruski-Corp Research." They paid him better than any other security gig in the past, so Teddy never bothered to question the secrecy surrounding the facility. He had been told they researched the subaquatic environment and the indigenous species of the Gulf, an explanation good enough for him. All he cared about was the medical benefits and the 401(k) 5% match.

The facility itself was unique in the way it was structured like a tree. The length of the "trunk" extended almost 2,000 fathoms. Each sector was a "branch" that stemmed out from the main body, eight in all. From afar, it resembled a tall oak floating in the ocean, but for some reason whenever Teddy glanced at photographs, the facility was no more elegant or beautiful than a baseball bat with eight nails sticking out of it.

As he stormed across the main lobby, pushing past people in white lab coats, he fiddled with the radio. Teddy struggled to locate a working channel. He ignored the many *hey!*s and *watch it!*s he received while knocking into almost every passing shoulder. Finally, he reached the elevator and prayed to the gods that it was operational. Five out of seven days, this wasn't the case. If any department lacked proper funding, it was maintenance.

Luckily, he caught the elevator at the right time of the week and the doors slid open before him. A few researchers exited, laughing at the punchline of a joke he hadn't heard. Once the elevator emptied, Teddy stepped on and immediately punched the button labeled for Sector 7. Outside, a few marine biologists were approaching the elevator with a little hustle. As the doors began to meet, Teddy heard one shout, "Hold the door!" He ignored them and felt bad doing so, but there was an emergency taking place, goddammit, and he had no time to waste on being polite.

The elevator grumbled and hiccupped the entire way down.

In less than thirty seconds, he arrived at Sector 7. Sweat poured from his brow as the doors parted and gave way to a long, rotund hallway, the size of a subway tunnel. A small, roiling wave of water rushed in, splashing over his feet.

What the...?

The water was ankle high. It sloshed back and forth inside the elevator like a miniature wave pool. Once the doors had fully opened, Teddy looked ahead, staring down the flooded hallway. He stepped into the dimly lit corridor. Sector 7—although primarily unoccupied—should've been lit like a Tokyo celebration. The disturbance seemed to have lowered the floor's operating power below 50%. Above him, the florescent lights flickered and buzzed, struggling to keep themselves alit.

Whatever happened down here, it was bad.

Teddy had never been down to Sector 7 since it was considered a "dead zone" and not much research took place here. Considering what he saw floating in the water, he suspected the seventh branch saw a lot more action than he'd been led to believe. Papers, folders, tables, chairs, writing utensils, a lamp, wooden shards that once belonged to a desk, and plastic food trays sailed on the ocean that now inhabited Sector 7. And...

Teddy froze. *Is that?*

Yes, it is.

A body. No more than fifty feet from the elevator, a solid, unmoving mass enveloped in a white lab coat floated across the corridor.

Teddy turned his head and placed the radio next to his ear. He listened intently and heard intermittent static and nothing else. Tired of the radio and its uselessness, he heaved it as far as he could throw. It sailed through the air and landed in the water twenty some yards away. It made a small splash before disappearing forever under the dark river.

Without the radio to distract him, his ears were attuned to new sounds. In the distance, he heard a noise that reminded him of childhood, when his mother would take him to the beach and he'd collect seashells. He remembered placing the seashells against his ear and listening to the ocean soundscapes within. Hearing it then brought him tranquility. Hearing it now—not so much. Quite the opposite. Something tugged at his gut, urging him to reconsider his duties here. To leave Sector 7 at once. To hand Pierre his two-week notice.

He ignored his gut and walked ahead cautiously, scanning his surroundings. He peered into each lab on his right and left. Every single room was unoccupied, now flooded. Computers and keyboards floated within, along with the occasional framed wall poster depicting various sea life. Interesting stuff Teddy might have stopped and admired under normal circumstances.

What the hell happened here?

Just when he asked himself that question, his gut acted back up, filling him with immediate dread. An idea struck him like a hammer to the base of his skull. *Get to the surface. Head to Sub-Level 3, grab Katie, take her to the submarine bay on Sub-Level 1, and break for the mainland.* They could be in Tampa in four hours, maybe less depending on the captain. He could be home, on the couch, catching up on his Netflix shows in no time at all. And more importantly, safe from whatever the hell was happening down here.

Before he could turn around, something cold crashed into his chest. The impact knocked him clean off his feet, sending him to the water below on his back. The water was ice cold and the arctic sensation crawled over his bones. Shivers cascaded down his vertebrae and danced across the muscles in his legs, numbing his extremities. Climbing back to the surface, he immediately sprung to his feet, rotating his entire body to see what had barreled into him.

A man wearing a shredded lab coat sprinted toward the elevator, spurts of red gushing from where his arm had previously been. His appendage had been ripped raggedly at the elbow. The scientist was panting like a dog on a hot summer day, struggling to keep his lungs full of air. He kicked up splashes of ocean water as he made for the elevator.

Teddy stared at the severed arm, eyeing every drop of blood that spilled from torn opening. He tried to look away but found he couldn't.

"Hey!" Teddy called to him. The man continued his pursuit of the elevator in ignorance. He reached the doors, held onto the large metal jamb for support, and started smashing the buttons with his one remaining hand. Teddy studied his face, the sheer terror that took hold. He'd never seen someone so scared before,

8

so...

...haunted.

Teddy wasn't so sure he wanted to see what made him that way. He positioned himself to run and waved his arms at the scientist, screaming for him to "hold the door!" Just like he had shut the marine biologists out on the main floor, the armless researcher ignored his request and Teddy watched his face disappear behind the closing metal slabs.

"Fucker!" Teddy shouted.

A temporary silence came, a prelude to the impending disaster.

Opposite the elevator, the ocean sounds roared. He turned and faced the dim cylinder-like corridor. The noise continued to build. Louder and louder until it reached crescendos, and then there was the constant sound of rushing, violent water.

A foamy white wall filled up the distance and it took Teddy less than a second to realize it was heading straight for him.

Teddy turned and bolted for the elevator. The knee-high water worked effortlessly to slow him down, something he didn't need considering his already-limited range of motion. He moved as fast as he could, as fast as his unfit body would allow, focusing on the unlit directional button mounted on the wall next to the elevator.

Behind him, a woman screamed. She sounded like a rooster at dawn.

Teddy glanced over his shoulder and saw a familiar face riding the foamy-white wave.

Katie.

What she was doing down in Sector 7, he had no idea. He froze, halfway between the elevator and the frothy swell.

"Katie?" he asked, refusing to believe his own eyes.

She screamed until her vocal chords broke. As the wave sped toward him, Teddy noticed the agitated rush wasn't just foaming white, but held a pinkish hue as well. As soon as he took notice of the wave's peculiar stain, the color sparkled with hints of cherry.

A shadow appeared behind Katie, and she found her voice again. A maw came next, slowly emerging in the colossal murk. The opened orifice advertised ivory daggers. The large mass began to materialize around her. Behind it, the fuzzy silhouette of an unknown beast, bigger than any animal Teddy had ever seen, land or sea. Bigger than anything he'd heard of, barring prehistoric monsters.

He reached out and cried her name. He knew what would come next, saw it play out in his mind before it happened. A part of him thought this was a bad dream and if he concentrated hard enough, he could wake himself up. It sure felt that way.

This can't be happening.

But it was. And Teddy witnessed the aquatic terror's toothy maw crunch down, mangling Katie's frame between them. The initial bite was as violent as he imagined, probably worse now that he'd seen it live and up close. Rivers of crimson merged with the white foamy wave. Katie's innards exploded outward, bursting forth like the guts of an overstuffed burrito. The mouth of the giant beast opened and closed several times, erasing more and more of Katie with each chew. Within seconds, she was reduced to fragments of flesh and bone and blood. Eventually there was nothing left of the girl except a splash of cranberry and Teddy's memories of her.

His tear ducts burned as the towering tidal wave crashed into him.

Wasn't long before an intense pain filled his body, clouds of red exploding across his vision.

It didn't last long, the pain nor the red.

In slithered a darkness that never let go.

1.

The grilled fillet of Chilean sea bass glistened in the late afternoon sun. The sweet, salty aroma of the bay was not enough to overpower the seafood scent. It was all around her. Jill McCourty gagged into her hand. To be polite she picked up her napkin and coughed into it. Her lymph nodes ached as bile crept up her throat. To avoid puking on her dinner date, she turned to the wine, the nearby glass of chardonnay.

Wine always made things better.

Well, not always, she thought, sipping from the glass. She wanted to kick back the entire glass in one swallow but she didn't think that would appear too ladylike.

"Not hungry?" asked the man sitting across from her. He already had a mouthful of swordfish steak. The next bite sat on his fork, sweating juices. He chewed like a man recently released from the state penitentiary. Judging from the childish artwork inked on his arms, Jill thought that was a major possibility.

"No, I am," she replied, resisting the urge to cover her plate with the napkin. "But I'm a vegetarian. I thought I included that tidbit of information in my profile."

The man in the trucker hat sporting gauged ears stopped chewing. "Really?"

"Mm-hm. I also believe the phrase 'looking to go vegan' was also in there, sooooo..."

Her date shrugged. "Can't say I know the difference between them."

Finally! A conversation starter! "Well, actually, vegetarians eat diary. Vegans don't eat anything that comes from animals. I've wanted to go vegan for a long time, only cheese is so—"

"You never, like, crave a steak?" He shoveled another lump into his mouth. "Filet mignon? London broil? New York Strip? Something juicy and dripping. Steak so soft it practically melts in your mouth?"

"Um. No. Gross." At this point she'd forgotten his name. Was it Brad? It could've been Brad. Brad sounded right. Maybe not. The longer the date dragged on, the less she cared. "I can't say I have." She almost added how its very mention made her nauseous but she bit her tongue. "Can we change the subject?"

"Sure thing." Another forkful of fish found his mouth. Some of it, however, missed the intended target and the white meat fell back to his plate.

Jill looked away, the man's poor table manners triggering her gag reflex. Sipping her wine, she looked past her date, out across the bay where her eyes settled on a billboard sign that read "Port St. Joe." The tranquil waters glittered where the sinking sun cast the day's last shine.

"So," he said, wiping his mouth with his collar. "What would you like to talk about, princess?"

Her heart thudded. She closed her eyes and listened to her inner voice shout, *Oh no he didn't.* It took every ounce of restraint to let the comment slip unaddressed. In the past this was not always the case. She had worked hard on letting the little things go. Her mother's dying wishes. Mom passed away last year after a long, spirit-crushing bout with cancer. Before the end, Jill promised she'd change her—as mother had put it—minor character defects. At the very least, she promised she'd *try.*

Try.

Keyword.

She took several deep breaths. It was important to remain calm. That was the first step. The second step was to smile. So she smiled. Not a great smile. Surely not her best. Just enough to let him know she was still interested. And she *was* still interested. Wasn't she?

Am I?

The patio restaurant wasn't overly crowded. Next to them, an old couple enjoyed their dessert, feeding each other mouthfuls of vanilla ice cream from across the table. It was adorable and she enjoyed spying on them, however the reluctant romantic in her doubted she'd experience a similar moment in her own life. Someone to grow old with. Someone she could connect with. Someone who *got* her.

You're only twenty-five, sweet pea, her mother's ghost whispered. *Still plenty of time!*

True, but with the long string of Neanderthals she'd been out with lately, the pool of hopefuls wasn't looking too promising. Plus, twenty-five wasn't all that young. Twenty-five was just five years to thirty and halfway to fifty. Scary statistics if she thought about it long enough, and sweet Jesus, she tried not to. It didn't help that most of her friends had already settled down, were either married or engaged. Shit, half of them had kids or were expecting. And yet, here she was. Grasping at straws on Meet-Your-Match-Dot-Com and a plethora of cheap (sometimes free) knockoff sites. She envisioned herself in ten years: still fiddling with dating sites, petting one of the twenty cats she'd probably adopt in a desperate state of lonely depression, consuming cozy mystery novel after cozy mystery novel, and bingeing on reality television while stuffing her face with bowls of cheddar-flavored popcorn.

Quite the life she planned out for herself.

Her date stared her, eyebrows arched, waiting for a response to a question he asked minutes ago. She noticed his plate was empty, not a single trace of his fishy dinner remaining.

"I don't know," she said, throwing her head back. The remaining wine went down like water. "What hobbies do you have?"

"Fishing, hunting, riding ATVs, four-wheelin'—"

She tuned out the rest of Brad's list. Slouching in her seat, she recalled all the television shows she needed to catch up on. She wondered if she appeared as disinterested as she actually was. At this point, she didn't care if her date recognized her complete boredom. She battled the temptation of excusing herself to the bathroom and bolting.

Her phone buzzed against the table.

Brad abandoned the conversation, finally noticing that listless look in her eye.

She glanced down at her phone, which had begun to chirp. FLORIDA STATE UNIVERSITY CALLING flashed up at her.

Her heart banged around in her chest; only one person would ever call her from that number. Jill bit her lower lip as she picked the phone up. "I'm sorry," she said to Brad without looking at him, her eyes glued to her iPhone. "I have to take this."

He didn't object.

"This is Jill," she answered, trying to sound professional.

"Hey, Jill!" a familiar voice answered, bright and chipper and full of hope. Hearing the voice was akin to having a razor dig into her heart. "Long time. How are you?"

She swallowed the knot in her throat. "Professor Pickard." With her teeth clenched together, she added, "How nice to hear from you."

"Jill, please. You know how much I hate Professor Pickard. Call me Neil."

"Ah. Right. Neil. Old habits die hard, I guess. Once a student, always a student."

"Did I call at a bad time?"

"No, now's fine," she said, eyeing Brad. He was looking around the patio for something else to fill his time.

"You sound annoyed," Pickard said, beating around no bushes. Before she could reply, he sighed noisily. "Look, I know things didn't exactly end peacefully between us, but I didn't call you to rehash old times."

"Why did you call, Neil?"

"I called as one professional to another." Silence for a beat. "I need help."

"Hm. Haven't heard that line, like, ever."

"Jillian, please—"

"Listen, pal. No one calls me Jillian except for my mother, and she's dead, so that leaves no one. Got it?" Pickard expressed his condolences. "Thank you. Now if you don't hurry this along and tell me why you're calling me after almost four years, I'm hanging up." She couldn't help herself and added, "I'm on a date."

"You're on a date?"

"Yes."

"Like... right now?"

"Yes, like right now."

"Wait, so you took my call during a dinner date?" There was a bit more humor in his voice than she cared for.

"Laugh it up, chuckle-nuts." She rolled her eyes. "If you must know, it's been a really terrible date."

Cocking his head, Brad looked at her with bewilderment. "But I thought we shared a connection?"

Neil snorted. "Wait, he's still there? In front of you? Oh, this is too yummy, Jill."

"Yeah, hold on, Professor," she said, grimacing. She pulled the phone away from her ear and cupped her hand around the lower half of it. "I'm sorry, Brad, but—"

"It's Ben," her date interjected.

"Brad, Ben, whatever. Look, this wasn't a good date. I know you think it was, but wasn't. Not even close. In fact, it's one of the worst dates I've ever been on. Actually scratch that—it *is* the worst date I've ever been on. Worse than the dude who brought his parents along and took the three of us to a raunchy comedy show. At least that was funny. This was just… well, terrible. Sad. Pathetic. Did I mention it was terrible? Okay, good. Just don't want to get our signals mixed. There won't be another date, Brad—Ben—sorry. But, hey. Chin up, kid. There's someone out there for you. I'm sure you'll settle down with a nice lady who enjoys shooting defenseless animals and gnawing on their bloody carcasses, or whatever you mountain men and women do nowadays. What was it? Riding…?"

"ATVs."

She snapped her fingers at him. "That's it. Yeah, that."

Silence fell over the table. Ben gaped at her.

"We're good," she told him. "You can run off now. Thank you for your time."

"But what about the check?" he asked, seeming concerned. "A man always pays."

"I got it, Brad," Jill said, waving him off. "No worries. We're square."

"It's *Ben,*" he corrected.

"Right. Ben. You're dismissed. Feel free to return to whatever cave you crawled out of."

Ben stood up. He rested his knuckles on the table and leaned forward. "You know what, lady? You're extremely rude."

"I know I am," she said apologetically. Her face scrunched as if something sour didn't sit well with her taste buds. "It's a disease, but I'm working really hard on getting that part of me fixed."

"Well, whatever you're doing, it ain't working."

"Thank you for the free personality assessment, Larry the

Cable Guy. Now..." She pointed to her phone before returning it back to her ear. "Some people," she said to Pickard as Ben threw his napkin down on the table and abruptly stormed out of the patio area. The surrounding tables had watched the whole scene unfold with growing smiles, except the old couple who continued feeding each other, grapes now.

Pickard returned to the phone, chuckling. "This has been the most interesting phone call ever," he said.

"You caught all that?"

"Oh yes. Recorded it, too. Uploading to Facebook as we speak."

"Fantastic."

"Classic Jill McCourty."

She narrowed her eyes while she chewed on a carrot stick, the only edible thing on her plate. "The hell is that supposed to mean?"

"Nothing, just... you haven't changed a bit."

"I disagree. I'm much smarter than we last met."

"Now that I believe." She heard him swallow hard, as if the words that came next had been stuck in his esophagus. "Listen, Jill. The reason I called..."

"Yes, please get to that."

"I really need your help on something, and I'd like you to come back to campus." He sighed, seemingly unready to hit her with the heavy news. "Preferably tonight."

She almost choked on the carrot. "Tonight?" She spat the orange stick out on her plate and ignored the dirty looks given by the surrounding patrons. "Get bent."

"Jill, I know it's been almost four years since we've spoken, but I wouldn't bother you like this if it wasn't extremely important. You're the smartest person I know, and honestly, I don't know who else to get involved. I really need your professional opinion on this."

"Flattery gets you nowhere, good sir." The waitress sauntered by. Jill rattled her empty wine glass in the air. The young woman came over inside of ten seconds and poured her another, smiling the whole time.

"Jill, this is serious stuff. I really need your help. I don't know who else to turn to."

She wondered how much more wine she needed to fall into his trap. "Hm, sure you don't."

Pickard released a breath of frustration. "I'm practically begging you here, Jill. Please. If you leave now you can be in Tallahassee a little after sundown."

She glanced at her watch. "How do you know I'm not in Miami about ready to get my party on?"

"Because I know you, Jill McCourty. I know you wouldn't leave Port St. Joe on a weekday."

"And why is that?"

"Because of your husband."

Jill laughed obnoxiously loud. Every head in the restaurant turned on her. Even the elderly. "Oh, Neil. You're funny. You could have at least done a little research before hitting me up for a booty call." More wine. A big gulp. She was starting to feel it. "I don't have a husband, Neil. I'm not married."

"Sure you are," he said confidently. "To the Port St. Joe's Sheriff's Department."

She rolled her eyes. "Good one, buddy. Were you waiting to whip that joke out the entire conversation?"

"More or less." He paused, dispersing air into the phone. "Like I said, Jill. I could really use your help. You're… the best student I ever had."

"I'm sure you've had better," she said, growing bored with this charade.

"Dammit, Jill. I'm trying to be serious here. I know you dropped out and never finished your marine biology degree, and I get it. Totally. You wanted to punish me by punishing yourself. Fine. In some strange way, I understand that. But can you put the past aside for five minutes and listen to me? I have something here and I don't know what it is. Before I go through the authorities and the proper channels, I thought you might want to have a look at it. Offer your opinion."

"Authorities, huh? Sounds serious."

"It is."

She kicked back the remaining wine. "Okay, Neil. Since I'm feeling generous," *and a little drunk,* she almost added, "I'll come have a look at your secret science project, whatever it is."

"Really?"

"Yes. But if this is some sick, manipulative ploy to arrange a face-to-face conversation with me about the past or our lives or the mistakes we made four years ago, then I will chop your sack off and feed your balls to the hungriest school of bull sharks I can find. Understand?"

She didn't wait for Pickard to respond. She hung up the phone and slipped it into her purse, then waved the waitress over and asked for the check.

"Extra mints, please," she said, forking over her credit card.

2.

The bottom trawl swung over the side of the boat and dropped on deck, spilling a sprawling mass of shrimp at the fishermen's feet. Under the setting sun, their catch's lustrous sheen sparkled like cut diamonds.

Dalton Earle, or "Duke" as his friends called him, had wide eyes as he looked over their biggest haul of the day. The smile that had broken across his face stayed there for a long while causing his cheek muscles to ache. He and his partner CJ took the hill of shrimp in with their eyes. CJ subdued his excitement while Duke pumped his fist as if he were in a New Jersey nightclub.

The grin on his partner's face was so wide that CJ thought Duke would surely strain something.

"We happy, boss?" Duke asked.

The twenty-five-year-old bent down on one knee for a closer look at their haul. He ran his eyes over the shrimp, wondering how much the trawl was worth. "Yeah, buddy. We're good. I'd say we're done for the day." He glanced at the western horizon. "Not much daylight left."

Duke nodded, his long, shaggy hair blowing back and forth in the late afternoon wind. He adjusted his cap to keep the loose auburn strands from bothering his eyes. "Sure thing, boss."

CJ squinted, tilted his head, and gave his first (and only) mate his patented look of disapproval. "What have I told you about the whole *boss* thing? It's weirding me out, man."

Duke chuckled. "Sorry, CJ. Just trying to nail down this whole boss-slave relationship thing we have going."

CJ rolled his eyes. "Dude, we're partners. Remember? This boat is mine just as much as it is yours."

Duke shrugged, continuing to flash his goofball smile. Duke and CJ were the same age, though Duke acted half that number a good portion of his day. There was hardly a moment that required him to remain serious. Not a major character defect in CJ's eyes, but from time to time Duke managed to get on a lot of people's nerves. CJ had been friends with him for so long that he'd gotten used to his antics.

CJ shook his finger. "If that's how it's gonna be, I'll start calling you Dalton."

Duke lost his smile instantly. "I'll throw myself overboard if that happens."

"Is that what it would take to get rid of you?"

"Oh yeah. For sure. But you wouldn't do that. You'd miss my funny jokes too much."

"But you don't have any funny jokes." Duke took pride in his humor and CJ knew the best way to knock him down a peg was to go after his comedic talent. "You're not funny. I mean, funny looking, sure. But not funny."

"Ha-ha. Leave the jokes to me, tough guy."

CJ couldn't argue with him. Duke was blessed with the comedic chops. In fact, when the two weren't fishing, Duke messed around with writing jokes and coming up with stand-up comedy routines, which he occasionally performed at local venues. In CJ's honest opinion, Duke's delivery needed a lot of work, but his friend had potential and the jokes themselves were funny as hell. He didn't go for those raunchy-for-the-sake-of-shock-value gags that seemed standard in today's comedy. His jokes were well thought out, a bit offbeat, and though he cursed on occasion, one would hardly consider him a "raunchy" comic. When he wasn't trying to keep his friend focused on the task at hand, CJ was actually supportive of his creative endeavors. He encouraged Duke to pursue comedy, especially when his friend went through those tough stages of reluctance and self-doubt.

For Duke, comedy was the dream. The reality: he was a fisherman, same as his best friend of almost twenty years.

Up until a week ago, CJ and Duke worked for Big Tom's Fishing Company, one of southwest Florida's most renown fishing lines. They'd been working for Big Tom every summer since they turned fifteen, although earning a measly seven bucks an hour would hardly be considered work by some. They had considered it borderline servitude. Their weekly pay was hardly worth the labor they tackled. And each dollar they did make went to future car payments and their college funds. Both of them came from lower-income families and their parents couldn't afford to send them to school. And they needed college because it was either that or working the docks for the rest of their lives. One demanding week at Big Tom's convinced them that the fishing life wasn't meant for them. CJ promised himself he wouldn't end up like the lifers at Big Tom's, guys like Woody Kearney, a raging alcoholic who cut more weekly child support checks than he could count on both hands, and Big Tom himself, a lonely, miserable prick who'd spent more time in court divorcing his fourth wife than at the helm of his moderately successful company.

Nope, he had wanted no part of that life.

But life doesn't always follow desired patterns, no matter how hard one tries, and CJ tried. If it weren't for his career-ending football injury in high school, he would've earned a full scholarship to Florida State. Senior year he tore his patellar tendon so badly the doctors needed several surgeries to properly install plating over the damage. They also braced his femur with a steel rod. The doctors told him his football career was over. Just like that. With one simple sentence his dream collapsed. Goodbye college, so long NFL, hello Big Tom's Fishing Company.

CJ convinced himself it wasn't all that bad. He went on to work full time for Big Tom over the next seven years and actually earned a decent living as a permanent employee. A far cry more than the high school students who just wanted a few extra bucks during summer vacation. The perks weren't all that great, but what he lacked in medical benefits and future-building portfolios, he made up with a decent salary and heavily discounted seafood. It was a good thing he liked shrimp and flounder because that was dinner five out of seven nights a week.

Not all bad, he thought.

It really wasn't.

That was until Big Tom's company went belly up. It seemed that the impending divorce with his fourth wife had wrecked him financially and a few weeks back, Big Tom informed his employees that he could no longer continue to pay them. Bad news for everyone who worked there, especially those old timers who'd had thirty-plus years' experience and were looking forward to retirement. But that was life, wasn't it? Always a curveball somewhere, a wrinkle in the sheets.

Instead of looking for work elsewhere, CJ and Duke pooled

their money together and bought their own commercial fishing boat. It was a bit of a gamble considering the price tag and the permits and the insurance, but they were able to make it work. CJ figured they'd live frugally until business picked up, but he was confident with the amount of connections he had made with local supermarkets and restaurants that they'd be able to secure enough sales accounts to get them by. It wouldn't be easy, but CJ set his goals on making back their expenditures and then some by the end of the calendar year.

CJ rose to his feet, his leg throbbing with pain and harsh discomfort. Despite his physical limitations, he tried to keep his body in good shape, hitting the gym four to five days a week. It wasn't an easy task, especially on days when the lower half of him rebelled. In those instances, he focused on shaping the upper half of his body, and because of this he had developed "chicken legs," giving his physique the shape of an upside-down pear. He couldn't help it. Some days it hurt too much to walk, let alone pump iron.

"You think Big Tom would appreciate today's pull?" Duke asked.

Peering into the deck freezer, they surveyed their inventory. It was a modest day's work. A few bluefish, some albacore tuna, a couple dolphin fish, and of course, the trawl of shrimp.

CJ grinned. "Knowing that fuck, probably not." He patted his friend on the back. "But it's good enough for us."

Being their own boss was kind of cool, but the responsibility was mentally taxing. Also, they had no established contracts and no clients to speak of. Not yet. CJ reminded himself they needed some inventory before they could hook clients, and they'd spent the week building one. Next week, he vowed to get out there and meet with potential buyers. He'd already begun practicing his salesman pitch. It wasn't very good, but he knew what he needed to work on. Besides, Duke was the people person. The sales aspect of the business would largely fall on his shoulders.

Lakes and rivers before bays and oceans, he reminded himself. *One step at a time.*

Even though they were close to broke and the future was unknown and scary, CJ was happy. For the first time in a long while, things were good. He was his own boss. He felt free.

Untethered. Frightened he might fail, but simultaneously content.

And shit, if it didn't work out, the local Costbusters was always hiring.

"All right," CJ said, "let's pack it in. Daylight's dying anyway."

Just above the horizon, the sun had melted into the sky behind a bulk of clouds, painting the previously blue expanse with strokes of lavender and swirling traces of tangerine. CJ stared at the beauty, recalling the infinite number of sunsets he'd seen over the years. He couldn't recall one more captivating than this. Then came an injection of pain directly into his kneecap. He doubled over and almost folded on the deck. He winced and pulled back in a crouching position.

"You okay?" Duke asked. CJ knew Duke recognized the symptoms.

The pain absconded quicker than usual. "Yeah. I'm fine. Fucking knee."

Duke shook his head. "You should get that shit looked at again. Not normal to have that much pain."

"Doctors said I'll have to deal with it for the rest of my life."

"Well, what do they know?"

CJ flashed a grin. "Rumor has it—everything?"

"Yeah, right." Sudden concern folded over Duke's face, which CJ found alarming. He was never this serious. "Can I ask you something?"

CJ nodded. "Yeah, buddy. Anything you want."

"Why not go back to school? Get an office job or something? Why did you go in on this boat with me?"

A bit surprised, CJ shrugged. "Fishing is all I know. Thought it'd be our best shot at making something of ourselves."

"It's just, you were pretty smart in school. You could have gotten a loan and paid for at least a few semesters of community college with the money we spent opening this business. I feel like you took the easy way out."

CJ wasn't used to serious conversations with Duke. In their lifelong friendship, conversations such as this only came around once every five years.

Duke put up his hands, surrendering to a fight that hadn't started. "I just don't want you to do this because of me. I don't want you to feel like you have to help me out because I'm not that smart. I know college isn't for me and without this, I'd likely be working dead-end jobs the rest of my life."

CJ waved him off. "You think I went in on this because I feel bad for you? Is that what you're saying?"

It was Duke's turn to shrug. He kicked a small bucket across the deck. "I guess."

"Uh, no. That's not the case. I told you, I don't want to go to college. That ship has sailed. This is my ship now."

"But why?"

"Why not?"

Duke rattled his head as if trying to shake out the courage to speak the truth. "Well, your physical condition for one."

"What does that have to do with it?"

"Come on, dude. I see the way you hobble around the deck. This life is killing you."

"It's not that bad."

"Don't bullshit a bullshitter." CJ opened his mouth, but Duke hushed him. "All I'm saying is that you should entertain the idea. Will you do that? For me?"

Duke winced as if an offensive odor passed by his nose. "Okay. Sure. Whatever you say."

There was a short period of silence, and in that moment— between the faint claps of waves—something knocked against the side of the boat. Something loud enough to cause the both of them to turn in the direction of the noise.

"What was that?" Duke asked. "Something hit us?"

"A dolphin?"

Duke shrugged. "Maybe. Bottlenose? The Gulf is full of them." Duke walked to the edge and peered below. CJ watched his friend's face pale the second his eyes fell on the source of the interruption. "Oh... oh shit."

"What's 'oh shit'? 'Oh shit' does not sound good." CJ limped to the edge of the boat, fighting off the shooting pain that trolled his leg. He sidled up next to Duke and followed his friend's gaze. Duke pointed at the object, but it was hard to miss as it floated beside the boat. "Oh shit," CJ said in exactly the same tone Duke had.

Next to their boat drifted an upper torso of what looked like a dead man in his early thirties.

"Tell me that's not a fucking dead body," Duke said. "Or what's left of one."

"That's not a dead body," CJ replied automatically. But it *was* a dead body and they both knew it. They saw a torn button-down shirt and ragged flesh floating within a copper cloud of blood. "Grab a net."

"What? You want to bring it aboard?"

Duke shrugged, unable to unglue his eyes from the nasty sight. "What choice do we have? We can't just leave it there. What if it's someone we know?"

"I don't get it," Duke said, running to grab the scoop net and the sturdy pole extender. "Where's the wreckage? If it were a boating accident, where's the boat?"

CJ shook his head. "Maybe it wasn't a boating accident."

He helped his friend lower the tool into the water and snare the body in the netting. The two of them lugged the torso up the side of the boat. The pole bent awkwardly and flexed to where they thought it might snap. Their catch was a hefty fellow and the water-logged death had probably added a few extra pounds to the weight. They managed the body aboard and dumped it on the deck, opposite the mound of shrimp.

Duke turned away, wishing they had explored the *let it lie* option more closely. CJ cut off the airflow to his nostrils and breathed through his mouth. The flavor of death found his tongue and he puked overboard, the crab salad he had eaten for lunch splashing to the ocean below.

"Disgusting, dude," Duke said, holding his own stomach as if that would keep it from revolting.

In the distance, something splashed on the surface, loud enough to grab their attention. CJ stumbled to the balcony and grabbed a pair of binoculars off the washboard. Peering out, setting his eyes on the surfaced object, he felt the rest of his lunch ascend.

"Oh God."

Duke jogged over. "What is it?"

"Another body."

"Are you shittin' me?"

"Nope." He handed him the binoculars. "See for yourself."

Duke waved him away. "Rather not. Seen enough for one day."

Below them, something splashed. Their eyes followed the sounds. No more than fifteen feet away, another object rose to the surface. A hazel brume surrounded the floater. This body was mostly intact; the man's shirt had been shredded open, revealing alabaster skin and bone-deep lacerations. They counted the man's limbs. None were missing. The ocean current began to escort the body away from them. Face down, the corpse sailed toward the horizon.

"Duke, get the line ready."

"You can't be serious."

"We might know him. Maybe we can help."

"We should call the coast guard. The local authorities."

"Okay, yeah. Do that. Meanwhile, I'll try to fish him out."

There was hesitation on both their parts.

Duke swallowed. "CJ, what the hell happened out there?"

As if the ocean had heard him, it sent another gift to the surface, this one mangled, its flesh torn to ribbons. A long strand of intestines rode in its wake, a swollen pink lanyard. Another body appeared twenty yards away, exhibiting similar wounds. Then another. Another after that, bobbing on the surface, riding the current. Then three at once, red clouds exploding around them like some underwater firework show.

Over the next minute, thirty bodies cruised to the surface, breaking the plane, turning the blue expanse into a watery graveyard of exhumed cadavers.

Then the boat lurched, sending CJ and Duke sprawling to the deck. Before they could recover, another jolt rocked the vessel, throwing them aside. Lumber cracked. Splinters the size of kitchen knives were sent airborne. Water rained down on them as some colossal shape broke through the surface, splitting their liner in two. Several waves crashed down on them, trapping the fishermen under the icy, unforgiving darkness of the ocean.

Before he went under, CJ noticed a large, obsidian fin cutting through the water. At first, he thought he'd seen a sailboat sporting a black sail. Upon closer inspection, it wasn't a sailboat. Or any other boat for that matter. It was a standard dorsal fin, although there was nothing standard about its dark color and tremendous size. It ran the length of a small car.

Next he spotted teeth.

Lots of those.

3.

Being back at the university did something strange to her body; she was barely able to stand when she climbed out of her car and it took a considerable amount of strength to push through the front doors of the campus's main administration building.

The guard stationed behind the desk barely looked up when Jill approached.

"Hi," she said to him, "I'm Jill McCourty. I'm here to see Professor Neil Pickard. He's expecting me."

The guard, no older than a student, glanced up from his book, *As I Lay Dying* by William Faulkner. "Campus is closed, ma'am. We don't let anyone into administration buildings past eight o'clock. I'll be happy to show you out."

"But he's expecting me," she repeated.

He smiled an obligatory smile. He'd clearly heard this song a thousand times before. "For your convenience, the library remains open twenty-four-seven, except on Sundays. Even has a coffee shop."

"That's great, but—"

"Ma'am," he said, putting his hands up in surrender. "I'm just doing my job."

"Okay, fine." She dug around the bottomless pit that was her purse. After a full minute of sifting through the crap, she wrapped her fingers around her shiny gold badge, her public shield. Dangling it in the security guard's face, she said, "Detective Jill McCourty. Sheriff's Department. Port St. Joe's. That do anything for you?"

With little emotion, the guard shrugged and said, "Not really."

She grunted, an oddly masculine sound. Before she could unleash her patented fury on the guard, she heard heavy footsteps clacking on the ceramic floor behind her.

"It's okay, Ryan," a familiar voice said calmly.

She turned and saw Pickard, looking as scholarly as ever. His green sweater was the color of baby shit and the hue alone made her nauseous. She debated asking him to take it off, which probably would have been taken out of context, thus opening a huge can of worms.

She kept her mouth shut.

Smiling, he adjusted his glasses to sit perfectly on his face. "Hey, Jill."

She smiled back, although he might have confused her greeting with the act of trying to unstick something from between her teeth with her tongue. If there were mixed signals, Pickard didn't say so. Instead, he gestured for her to follow with a wave of his hand.

"Come with me," he said.

She followed him down the hallway but not before sticking her tongue out at the guard, who had already returned to his literary assignment, no longer concerned with protecting the administration building from unauthorized visitors.

"This better be good, mister," she said, trailing Pickard down the hall. "I have work tomorrow."

He looked over his shoulder and shot her a conniving smile. "You're probably going to want to call in a personal day."

"Has anyone told you your sweater looks like baby shit?"

He ignored her and turned the corner, leading them down another corridor. Half the lights were out and Jill figured the university was just cutting back on expenditures. The farther they walked, the darker their surroundings became. An absurd notion came over Jill, one that detailed Pickard luring her down into a dungeon where he and his old frat buddies would assault her sexually and carve her body into several pieces after they finished. She pushed those malicious thoughts aside, cursing herself for being so unnecessarily gross. She tuned her mind into pleasant reflections: sleeping on the couch till noon, her affectionate cat Lumpy, and a bottle of Dry Creek.

"Sorry for the long walk," Pickard finally said, bringing the run of silence to an end. "As you can see they moved my lab. I think it was retaliation for some disagreements with the board, but you know—can't prove it, so…"

She flashed him a grin, pretending she cared.

After a few more paces, they reached an elevator.

"Going down?" she asked.

He stepped on, pressed the button with a giant "B" on it, then nodded.

"Oh, great," she said, following his lead. "You don't plan on killing me, do you?"

Pickard laughed. "Jill…"

Well, he didn't say no, she thought.

As the elevator doors closed and a bell sounded, Pickard turned to her and put his back against the dull, tarnished, metallic wall. "You seem well. Happy even. That's good." For the first time since she was twenty-one, Neil Pickard was close enough to kiss. "I don't want to open old wounds, but if it's any consolation, I'm sorry for what happened. If I could change things, I would."

She shook her head. "Not here to talk about the past, Neil. I came to see whatever's in your basement and then I'm out."

"Well," he said, folding his arms. "I have a feeling that might change once you see what I've got."

She couldn't help but view his smile as creepy. The gang-rape scenario played out in her mind and she internally scolded herself for being such an idiot. A sudden rush of regret penetrated her bones and the urge to punch the emergency stop button on the control panel jumped her. It took everything in her power to quell that impulse.

"Please don't kill me," she said, closing her eyes.

He burst into laughter. "Are you serious?" he asked, the question bookended with a series of chuckles.

She arched her eyebrows.

"God, you're serious." His laughter died along with his smile. "No, Jill. I'm not going to kill you. Don't be absurd."

A wave of relief washed over her. "Good. Because, you know, I have, like, work in the morning. And if you were to kill me, someone would know."

The elevator doors opened and she followed him out, down another dark hallway. She thought she'd seen this hallway before in a John Carpenter flick. The fluorescent lights flickered above, the ones that hadn't run out of juice, which weren't many. The floor was filthy and riddled with prints of muddy footsteps. Cobwebs infested the corners where the wall and ceiling met. It appeared no one but Pickard ever came down here.

In about twenty feet, they came to a door with "Professor Cornelius Pickard" etched in the glass, bold collegiate lettering.

He opened the door and invited her in, into the pitch dark. Hesitantly, she stepped inside, bracing herself for the grabbing arms, the trap she envisioned since her arrival. Once the both of them were inside, the lights kicked on. She was relieved to find it was just the two of them.

Well, technically they weren't alone.

On the gurney in the center of the room lay a cadaver. There was a dark green bag over it, less puke-green than Pickard's sweater and more of a leafy sort.

Pickard summoned her over. Whatever he wanted her to see drew a faint smile on his face.

"You brought me all the way to Tallahassee to show me you've taken up necrophilia?" She shook her head. "Always knew you were a sick son of a bitch. Guess I have to arrest you now."

His smile widened. "I always did look good in handcuffs."

"Okay, too far. Gross. Dead bodies I can handle, but anecdotes on your sex life—that's where I draw the line, pal."

He waved her over again, more emphatically this time. "Come look."

Skeptically, she set her bag down on a nearby table and drifted over to him. He handed her a mask. She placed the band over her head and adjusted the mask so it covered her nose and mouth. He nodded as if to say, *Hold onto your butt, here we go!*

He unzipped the body bag. The green plastic gave way to a man in his early thirties, his complexion a milky white that almost seemed artificial. Dark blue tributaries of veins were spread across his skin, some as thin as spider web silk, some swollen, as thick as a drinking straw. Contusions of varying degrees marred the corpse, looking like someone had beaten him like a pinata in the closing moments of his life. His lips were dark, a midnight blue. Jill had seen about a dozen cold bodies over her four years at the Sheriff's department, but still hadn't gotten used to the soulless gaze of the dead. After a while, she had to look away.

"Did he die from asphyxiation or trauma?" she asked, her eyes running over the purple bruises plaguing the flesh.

"Undetermined. But both, my guess."

"Okay, so who is he and where did you find him? And more importantly, why is he here and not in a morgue?"

"One question at a time," Pickard replied. He spun on his stool and faced her. "His name, according to the security badge we found pinned to his shirt, is Theodore McDermott. He washed up on Sharkwater Beach this morning."

"Sharkwater Beach? Isn't that part of Key Water Island? That section of the beach the school owns?" She knew the island. Knew it well. It was where Pickard had taken her on many unsanctioned "school projects."

"Yes. *That* island. I'm actually surprised you forgot about it. It was where—"

"Okay, okay, okay. I remember. No need to reminisce. Just get to the part that involves me. Tell me why I'm here." She nodded at the stiff. "And about our buddy Teddy. Why isn't he with the local authorities?"

Pickard shrugged like a kid who had knowingly done some wrong, but wouldn't fully own up to it. Instead, he responded, "Sharkwater Beach technically lies in international waters. This body doesn't really belong to anyone."

"Um," Jill said, looking up at him. "You said he had a security badge? Surely the company he works for—uh, sorry, *worked* for—would disagree with you. As would the good old boys in the Tallahassee Sheriff's Department when they find out you've assumed the role of coroner in these parts."

"Jill, it's not like that. I—"

Jill didn't want to hear it. She stopped him by thrusting her palm forward. "Neil, what the hell were you thinking?"

He gave no response.

"Does anyone know about this?"

He shook his head.

"Good. Well, we'll just bring it back to the beach and dump it there. Let someone else discover it for the first time. I can help you."

Again, Pickard's head swung side to side. "No, Jill. You don't understand."

"No, *you* don't understand. How the hell were you going to explain this to the police? Trust me, the finders-keepers excuse, the 'I-borrowed-this-dead-guy-in-the-name-of-scientific-research' story will not go over well. You'll be their number one suspect faster than you can blink."

"Jill, I love you. But you need to close your mouth."

Love me? Those two words filled her with a rage she hadn't felt in a long time. Pain crawled up her arms. Her cheeks burned. The room began to look a little lopsided. She wasn't sure if she was entering a fit of blind rage or having a panic attack. Both were not welcome.

She almost told him to fuck himself or the corpse he'd stolen, but she managed to keep those words locked up. A temporary moment of inner peace washed over her, and the burning discomfort on her skin slowly faded.

I love you, he had said. She knew he didn't mean it the way he once did, but still, it was the wrong fucking thing to say.

"Okay, I'm sorry," he said, noticing the sudden change in her complexion. "I shouldn't have said it. Poor choice of words."

Jill bit her tongue until the taste of copper ran bold. "No sweat. The past is in the past. I'm over it."

He looked at her, seemingly unconvinced, but he didn't press the matter. "Good. That's good." He returned his focus to the cadaver. "Look at this." He pointed to Theodore's belly. Here, things were a little gruesome. Something had torn through his flesh and muscle, the skin surrounding the twelve-inch gash so purple it was almost black. Most of his entrails had been excised, and his stomach had been reduced to a bloody pocket of mush. It reminded Jill of a smashed potato.

"What am I looking at?" she asked.

"You don't see them?"

"Them?" She leaned in and gave the open cavity a better look. After fifteen seconds of the same disgusting scene, Pickard assisted the search by directing her eyes to a small army of black specks invading a portion of Theodore that looked like a deflated balloon. Jill guessed that was the man's liver. The little black dots crawled over the pinkish-white surface, busy little clusters that scurried like ant hordes, only with no calculated purpose.

"What is that shit?"

"I don't know," Pickard said, shrugging. "Nothing I've ever seen before. They were already embedded in him when we retrieved him from the shore."

"We?" Jill's eyes bulged. "I thought you said no one else knows about this?"

Pickard turned on his schoolboy charm and smirked. "A few students were with me. But they are cool, Jill. I promise. They won't speak a word of this to anyone."

Jill swallowed all the names she wished to call him. She really wanted to punch his face off.

He turned his attention back to the cadaver and the small black specks. "Whatever they are, they came from the ocean."

"They look like ants. Or little spiders."

"Ever hear of a water spider before?"

"Diving Bell Spider. They live almost entirely underwater."

"In Europe. In freshwater. Not in the Gulf." Pickard huffed. "Besides, Diving Bells are much bigger. These things are practically microscopic."

"I don't know. Maybe it's some parasite."

"Jill, no. I've kept the body clean. I even used formaldehyde. These things were living inside him. Underwater."

"Did your run tests?"

"Minimal. Far as I can tell, these little guys' DNA don't match anything found in our waters. Or in the world. Not even close."

"Okay, so you got me. I give up." Jill stood up and threw her arms apart. "Can I go home now?"

Pickard didn't hide his disappointment. "You're not the least bit interested?"

"In a bottle of wine—yes. In small, ocean-dwelling creepy-crawlies? No. Can't say that I am." She checked her watch. "Sooooo, this has actually been the most fun I've had on a date in a long time. Thank you, Neil. You sure know how to make a lady feel special."

"Jill, there's something else I need to show you."

"Oh, Jesus. You're not going to whip out your wiener, are you?"

Pickard slumped his shoulders. "Can you be serious for once?"

She kept hush on the subject, making no promises.

Pickard turned and headed for another table in the corner of the room. He opened a drawer and removed an object that looked like a giant triangle. Holding it with both hands, he returned to the center of the room, presenting it like a newborn baby.

"Take it."

Reluctantly, she reached for it with both hands. "What is it?" she asked, although deep down, she knew.

"It's a tooth." The bone-white triangle passed between their hands. "Which, best as I can tell, came from a big-ass shark."

The size of the tooth took up both palms. "Big-ass shark? Is that a new species or something?"

"Didn't come from a Great White. Their teeth are much smaller."

"No kidding." A Great White tooth was three inches maximum. This was almost four times that. "If this thing is real, we're talking Megalodon territory."

"It's real," Pickard said, almost defensively. "And think larger because a Meg tooth is six, seven inches tops." He pointed to the abnormality in Jill's hands. "That measures almost twelve."

Jill looked up from the tooth and studied her former professor. "Neil, where on earth did this come from?"

Pickard jerked his shoulders. "Sure wasn't the Gulf of Mexico. Hell, I'm not even sure it came from this planet."

4.

Darkness all around her. And food. She felt the vibrations bouncing through the deep, the slightest displacement of water overloading her senses. Now that she was free, her perception of the world sharpened. This new world swam and danced around her, the all-encompassing fluid sparkling with life. It was perpetual chaos at its finest.

Schools of fish darted in the opposite direction as she glided through the deep. Hammerhead sharks, fierce in their own right, avoided her colossal mass at any cost, diving to depths they normally wouldn't swim. This came as a surprise. She thought there would be some sense camaraderie amongst the sharks of this world. But there was none. Not a soul in the ocean wanted anything to do with her. She was treated like a plague. In some ways she was.

One thing was definite: she was on her own out here.

An eternal hunger yearned for sustenance. The humans didn't know how to properly feed her; they knew nothing about her whatsoever. If they had, they wouldn't have kept her tethered. They would have killed her. Should have killed her. They had failed as her caretaker, not knowing how much food her system required to function. An impossible amount. But no worries. She was free now. Free to feed as she pleased.

The humans weren't completely useless. Upon her escape, they proved helpful, nourishing her like no meal in the past. She devoured meat and bones, swam playfully in the ocean of blood she had created on her violent exit.

As she glided through the deep, she felt something move inside her. Her belly wriggled with a certain discomfort. There was something else occupying her body, but what, she could only speculate.

Life?

Was she...?

She didn't remember going through a pregnancy in her former life, no memory of giving birth whatsoever.

What did the humans do to her?

Tests.

Many tests.

An incalculable amount.

They had poked and prodded her, injected her with their secret serums. All in the name of science, they said, although she didn't know what that meant. She guessed she could be pregnant. The humans could have planted the seed inside her as part of their experiment.

She had an enigmatic notion to head toward land, which seemed ridiculous because sharks and land were like oil and water. But alas, the body received what the body craved. She knew that. That was knowledge she learned thousands of years ago, a time filled with darker and sinister outlooks, when each day was a constant struggle for survival.

She rose rapidly and cruised below the break. Cresting the surface, her dorsal fin cut through wind and water. She moved slowly in case she crossed another human vessel. When stalking prey, the element of surprise was crucial, especially on this planet. Below the water, at night, she was invisible to plantigrade creatures from above the surface.

Killing was fun, the entire process overly gratifying. Most sharks killed for sustenance only. Now she was eating for four and, yes, sustenance was integral, but there was nothing greater than the intense satisfaction she garnered watching exploding red clouds appear before her, billowing in the dark water. Each violent assassination elated her. Filled her with purpose. Gave her more stimulation than the nourishment that followed.

It was impossible to understand all these feelings, these conflicting emotions. Sharks weren't meant to feel such things. Sharks operated on instinct, millions of years worth of natural proclivity. They lived out their days according to the structure of their DNA. Nothing less, nothing more. But not her. She operated on how man tampered with her already alien DNA. She acted on the impulses they planted inside her. She made her own choices now, basing her decisions on how she felt, not what nature dictated.

She was the queen of the ocean now. And anything in her way would find out exactly what that implied.

Head for land, *a little voice told her.* There will be food. *Land sounded like the perfect idea—an all-you-can-eat buffet.*

5.

For a solid twenty minutes they sat down at Pickard's desk and made small talk. They danced around the elephants in the room, their rocky past and the dead guy harboring an unknown parasitic membrane. Questions on both topics brewed within Jill's thought pool, none of which Pickard would answer. On the parasite end of things, nothing made sense. The only thing for certain was that Pickard had discovered a new species. Something that shouldn't exist. Then there was the giant shark tooth. Another anomaly. No shark on the history of the planet had ever been that massive. Given the tooth's size she estimated the sea beast to be around one-hundred-feet long. Maybe more. It was hard to imagine a gargantuan creature of that length.

"Are you sure it's real?" Jill asked. "I mean, maybe your students are messing with you. Playing a gag on the *cool* college professor because he can take a good joke."

"For the fifth time, yes, it's real. Calcium levels are through the roof." Pickard dropped his elbows on the table. His chin rested on folded hands. His face was long and wiped clean of color, pale from lack of sleep and the dread of their discovery. "Jill, what do we do?"

"You're asking me?" She laughed incredulously. "I don't know. You're the professor."

"About the body, I mean."

"Oh, well that. I told you. Dump it. Let someone else deal with it."

"But the discovery… What it would mean."

"Then keep it, Neil. I don't give a shit." She glanced down at her watch—2:00 a.m. The realization of how late it was brought forth a yawn. She stretched her arms. "I'm exhausted. I have work in four hours. If I leave now, I can—"

"Stay," he said. The look on his face frightened her. Not because he was mad, but because he was scared. Unnerved beyond rational thought. She'd never seen Professor Cornelius Pickard look anything other than confident, and the face across from her caused her skin to ripple with gooseflesh. "Please."

She stared into his eyes for a long time. She counted the seconds. Sixty of them total. It took that long to remember the flame they once shared had long since flickered out. There was no chance of rekindling. She knew that. Too many bad memories, too many unforgivable circumstances.

In that moment she witnessed a sensitive side to Pickard she hadn't remembered. Pain welled in the big brown circles of his eyes. Pain… and something else.

"Neil…" she said, almost breathless.

"Please?" He asked this time, sounding like a child who wanted one more spin on the merry-go-round. "I don't want to be alone with… whatever this is. You're the only one I can trust, Jill."

"And why is that?" She arched her eyebrows.

"Because you could have buried me a long time ago. You could have filed a complaint with the university."

Valid point.

She bit the inner skin of her cheek. "If this is some sleazy attempt to—"

He raised his hand. "It's not. Jill, I promise you, it's not. Just… shit, I can't go to the authorities. You're right. They'll lock my ass up. The university will fire me immediately, especially considering how I've ruffled a few feathers lately, and my career will undoubtedly end."

She explored his thoughts. He wasn't wrong. She could corroborate his story, but that would only put the both of them behind bars and next in line for a county straightjacket the second they started talking about hundred-foot sharks. Even with proof their story would be difficult to authenticate. It would take forever for the police to conduct a proper investigation, sift through their findings, and clear them of charges. Well, not forever, but at least a few days to a week. She could make a few phone calls, of course, pull a few strings, but it would cost her. Her near-perfect reputation might become tarnished and she couldn't afford that.

"Okay," Jill said, rubbing her eyes with her knuckles. "Let me think." There wasn't much to think about. They had a body and they needed it gone. "We have to hide the body. We have to. No other choice here."

He shook his head. "We need to preserve the discovery."

"This *discovery* will cause you more headache than it's worth. Do I need to explain the procedure when you call the police and tell them you've been conducting research on a dead body you happened to find on the beach?"

"In international waters," he reminded her.

"Irrelevant." She pouted her lips like an ornery child. "Do I?"

"No, you don't."

"Good. Now, you said you found a security badge on him?"

He nodded.

"Let me see."

Pickard shuffled through a stack of files on his desk. Underneath the ungraded research papers and outlines of next semester's itineraries rested a Ziploc bag. The man's identification was safely sealed inside. As she covered her hands with latex gloves, he slid the bag across the table.

"I hope to Christ you had the good sense to keep your fingerprints off this," she said, cracking open the plastic strip and retrieving the card inside. Crusty black dots speckled the inside of the Ziploc and the card itself. Some of it flaked off as she handled the ID. She *hoped* it was the man's blood and not the tiny lifeforms that had pillaged the dead man's innards.

"Of course," he said. "I'm not a complete moron."

She grinned. "I'll be the judge of that, buddy." She examined the badge, flipping it over. On both sides, a company name and logo was inscribed in the top right corner. "Petruski-Corp," she read aloud. "Never heard of them."

"Me neither."

"Did you research it?"

Putting a crinkle in his brow, he replied, "No. Should I have?"

Jill exhaled dramatically and shook her head. "Some detective you are."

"But I'm not a detective."

"And thank the good Lord for that." She pushed a stack of books aside so she could access his MacBook Pro. "Any porn on here you don't want me looking at?"

Pickard squinted at her.

"Oh, stop. Lighten up, dude." A grin overcame her face. "You should count yourself lucky. This is the first personal day I've taken since... well, ever."

"And I appreciate it. But can we keep the jokes to a minimum?" Pickard snatched a candy bar out of the desk drawer, peeled back the wrapper, and stuffed the chocolaty treat in his mouth. "I find this situation incredibly stressful and far from funny."

"Hey, wherever I go, so do my jokes. It's a small price to pay for my company." She winked at him, but not in a *hey-I-think-you're-cute* way. At least she hoped that's not how it came across. "I have this memory of you being the cool professor, the one everyone on campus requested as soon as registration opened. Shit, I remember you had accounting majors taking Analysis of Ocean Ecosystems just to listen to your lectures. I guess what I'm getting at is—when exactly did your balls drop off?"

He didn't respond. Instead, he sucked his lips and stared at his candy bar as if it had cast the insult.

"Okay then." Jill cleared her throat. "Moving on. According to the Internet—AKA a detective's best friend—Petruski-Corp is a small American company that specializes in biological testing. They're operated by a parent company that does pharmaceutical engineering, mostly in the field of researching deadly diseases. Cancer. Alzheimer's. AIDS. Ebola. The list goes on." She spun in her chair and faced Pickard. "Looks like these guys are fighting the good fight. Real-life heroes trying to make a difference. Trying to save the world one pill at a time."

"I doubt it."

Jill snorted. "Yeah, they're probably in it for three Fs—funds, fame, and fucking."

"Okay, this is great information and all, but does this explain how our friend Theodore ended up on Sharkwater Beach with a prehistoric tooth lodged in his ribcage?"

Jill pulled her lips to one side and snapped her fingers, the worst Elvis impression she could muster. "You know it, baby." She held up the badge six inches from his face. "See that? Says S.Q.U.I.D." Then she highlighted the words next to the acronym with her finger: Security Team.

The professor shrugged. "So? What does that mean?"

"Don't know, and neither does Google. So that leads me to believe our unfortunate friend Teddy here was up to some shady shit." Grimacing, her eyes fell on the guard's face and studied his features. They hardly matched the corpse on the slab. If Jill didn't know the guard had been found with the badge on him, she'd say they were two different people. "Well, not Teddy himself. But his company definitely is. Petruski-Corp Research." She turned back to the laptop and started clicking the mousepad. "Their website is bare bones. Almost as if they're hiding something. Very *fishy* to me." She smiled, looking back at Pickard over her shoulder. "Get it? *Fishy.*" She waited for his reaction but got nothing. "You know. Because we're, like, dealing with fish. Sea stuff. Sharks. Fish. Funny, right?"

He glared at her, his face still as a slab of stone.

She clicked her tongue and jabbed his chest with her forefinger. "You're no fun."

For the next several minutes, she scoured the Internet. When she came up empty, she swung herself away from the laptop. She rubbed her neck while stretching her arms and back.

"Look, I got a theory," she said, finishing her stretch and folding her arms across her chest.

"This ought to be good."

"Hang in there with me. What if this Teddy dude was working at some research station in the Gulf somewhere?"

"In the Gulf? What, on some super-secret island? We'd know about it if that were the case."

"You're right. Too conspicuous. Unless it wasn't an island. Unless..."

"What?"

"Unless it was underwater."

"An underwater research station? Is it me, or this starting to sound like a *Sharknado* movie?"

"It's you." She raised a single forefinger in the air. "Let's say there is a facility out there, below water, maybe a few thousand fathoms from the surface. Let's say something happened there. Maybe it was attacked by our toothy friend. Body washes on Sharkwater Beach several days later and there we have it."

Pickard didn't look impressed. He sucked in a long breath and tossed the empty candy wrapper in the garbage. "That's a wonderful theory, but you're forgetting one thing."

"What's that?"

"That it doesn't really matter where Teddy came from. What matters is that we have a giant shark out there that shouldn't exist in nature. I mean, what if it heads to the mainland? To our beaches?"

Jill moved her shoulders in a slow shrug. "What are *we* supposed to do about it?"

"Find it. Track it down. Before it kills more people."

"How do you suppose we do that?"

"I thought that's why I called you."

Jill laughed out loud in a pitch that surprised herself. "Listen, Neil. You need me to find some scumbag who broke into your house and stole your television set, I'm your girl. Giant fucking shark from the Mesozoic—well, I don't know who you call for that. Ghostbusters maybe, but one can't be too sure when dealing with giant sharks."

"Again with the jokes."

Jill's smile faltered. "I don't hear you offering up any suggestions."

"Actually," he said, grabbing three folders off a nearby pile of paperwork. "I do." He opened the folders and laid them down on the desk.

"What's this?" She glanced down and read the heading: Consent Form. They were each signed and dated at the bottom. One signature by Professor Cornelius Pickard, the other three by his students. "Oh. I remember these."

"Special research trip to Sharkwater Beach. Approved by the university, of course. It's late August and the bull shark population has increased. It's time for their annual feeding frenzy. The perfect cover. I hand-selected my best students."

"Best or favorite?"

He bit his lip and flared his brow. "Both. Besides, they were with me the other day when we found Theodore. We were doing a bit of preliminary scouting."

She read the names. "I see two out of the three are girls. Banging any of them?"

Pickard's face went slack. "That was a low blow."

"Thought you liked low bl—" She stopped herself, realizing she'd taken things a little too far. She choked down the rest of her sentence and nodded. "Yeah, sorry about that. Guess I got a little carried away."

He let out a breath so deep it sounded like he'd held it for hours. "Guess I sort of deserved it, didn't I?"

She nodded. "Yeah. I mean, you kind of did."

Silence settled between them. When she couldn't stand it anymore, she stood up from the stool.

"So I guess that's it then. Good luck with your little shark hunt—"

"You're coming with us," he said, as if it was already decided.

"Um, say what now?"

"You're coming with us," he repeated in the same confident tone.

"No. I told you. I have a job. I can't just take off to go hunt Jaws. I'm sorry, Neil. I can't."

"Jill, we're on the brink of discovering something truly epic. Something no one on this planet has ever seen before. Whether it's a giant shark or these small black parasites, we're going to uncover something new. This is a marine biologist's dream."

She nodded. "A *marine biologist's* dream. Not mine."

"You would have been one. Damned fine one if you ask me."

She closed her eyes.

"What happened to the eager college student I once knew?" Waiting for a response, he leaned back in his chair and folded his hands against the back of his head. "Where'd she go?"

"A professor killed her, I think. Smashed her heart into a million pieces."

He nodded as if he understood perfectly. "I wish she'd come back."

"Hm. I bet you do." She moved away from the desk and headed to where she left her purse near the door. "I really gotta go, Neil."

"What happened to that personal day?" he asked, rising to his feet.

She shrugged. "Haven't called it in yet. If I leave now, I can make it back in time for a shower and a cup of coffee."

"Jill, I'm begging you here. Do I have to get down on my hands and knees?"

She scratched an itch just below her hairline. "Amusing as that would be, no."

"I'm sorry for the pain I caused you. A thousandfold. But I can't take back what happened between us. I can't change what I did. I'm an asshole. I admit it. What happened was completely my fault. But I've learned a lot since then. I've gotten better. I'm not that asshole anymore."

"I'm happy for you, but I'm still not going on a tropical vacation with you."

"I need you, Jill. And not romantically. I need you with me. On Sharkwater Beach. I need the best student I ever had. The student you were, and the detective you are now." He chewed on his tongue while mustering the courage to speak on. "Plus, it would help to have a member of the police force on hand. You know. With a gun, in case things get hairy."

"Are you kidding me?"

He closed his eyes. "Please, Jill. I know you don't owe me anything, but... I don't know who else I can turn to."

She sighed with frustration.

"Don't you want to know what Petruski-Corp Research is? What S.Q.U.I.D. is?" He pointed to the stiff on the gurney. "Who Theodore was?"

Deep down, her curiosity raged—the other character flaw her mother always warned her about. Curiosity caused her a lot of trouble as a small child, something mom always assumed she'd grow out of but never did.

"What do you say?" Pickard asked, wincing, fearing her answer.

She rolled her eyes. "Well, I never could say *no* to you."

The lower half of Pickard's face was all teeth.

6.

The chopper circled the wreckage under the mask of night. Out here, fifty miles from the coast, they weren't at risk of being seen. Not at three in the morning. Plus, according to their coordinates, these waters were considered international. They belonged to no one. Occasionally the DEA policed them, attempting to thwart drug runners exporting large shipments from Mexico, but those instances were pretty rare, at least in Brinks's experience. The cartels usually paid good money to keep those ocean lanes clear and unless someone had forgotten to settle a bill, he suspected they wouldn't run into any hassles tonight. Plus, if for some reason the DEA did show up, they wouldn't bother a military-grade chopper with the star-spangled banner branded on its shell.

"I'm dropping her down to twenty feet!" the pilot yelled over the rhythmic clicking of the blades above.

The man in the passenger's seat, built like a small bulldozer, gave him the thumbs up. The two men sitting in the back armed with assault rifles slapped each other high five. Champing at the bit for a little action, neither one of them could keep their asses still. They squirmed in their seats and pumped their legs as if they were riding a bicycle.

The pilot dropped them down without ease and the chopper bucked, knocking the passengers around.

"Jesus!" Brinks shouted, looking over at the pilot. He tapped the son of a bitch on the shoulder. "What the hell are you doing?"

The two passengers in the back snickered. One of them cleared his throat and asked, "Where did Petruski find this asshole?"

"Sorry, sir!" the pilot responded. Sweat poured down his face. Under his helmet was like a sauna, a film of condensation clinging to his visor. "I'm not used to these amphibious helis!"

"Well you better learn pretty fucking quickly!" Brinks chided him over the rapid *tk-tk-tk* of the propeller. "Set her down over there!"

"Sir?"

Brinks pointed to an empty stretch of water between two hunks of floating metal. He raised his thumb at the pilot again.

"Too close to the wreckage!" the pilot snapped. "We could bust the landing skids up!"

Brinks closed his eyes and corralled his anger, a task that proved awfully difficult time and time again. "I wasn't asking permission, asshole! I said land the fucker! Over there!" He jabbed his forefinger in the direction of the targeted landing area.

The pilot remained silent while the helicopter hovered over the Gulf. Ten seconds passed before the pilot smiled and blurted out, "You got it, sir!"

Brinks felt his stomach leap into his throat during the quick descent. He had experienced "rough landings" before, but this was absurd. He figured Petruski had put the pilot on payroll the second he flunked out of flight school.

Our mystery boss's funds must be drying up, he thought.

Had he known the pilot was slightly suicidal, Brinks would have offered to fly the chopper himself.

He turned and poked his head in the back seat, giving his boys a quick nod. "You crazy sons of bitches ready?"

Gardner, the big black man on the left, formed an O with his mouth and bellowed, "Hoorah!"

Hanson, the scrawny redneck sporting a blond handlebar mustache, pumped his fist in the air and hollered, "Yeehaw!"

Brinks loved them like brothers. The three of them had been through some shit together, seen things that might break the mind of an ordinary man. But not the Goon Squad. They were cut from a different cloth. Between four tours in Afghanistan and several "dark" missions in Syria, Baghdad, and Paris, the trio had formed a unique bond, cemented by blood, fear, and the ultimate rush of the near-death experience. They were more than partners or co-workers, fellow soldiers; they were brothers born together in the United States military. A bond that wasn't so easily broken.

But that was then. A lot had changed since they were honorably discharged. Now they worked freelance jobs, ready to hire as long as the price was right and the job was worth it.

They recently became exclusive employees for Petruski-Corp Research. Small jobs. Nothing too dirty. Intimidation games mostly. Shakedowns. Reminding people who owed Petruski money that they, in fact, still owed Petruski money. Some were more forgetful than others. Some needed the information beaten into their skulls or scarred on their skin. Pain helped people remember, a lesson Brinks and the Goon Squad knew all too well.

Petruski paid well and Brinks and his men liked the money almost as much as they enjoyed the work. The jobs were menial and the checks always cashed. Over a short timeframe, Brinks grew suspicious of how easy they had it, figuring it wouldn't last long. Sooner or later, Petruski would call in a "favor," ask them to get their hands dirty or involve them in something that wasn't mentioned during the orientation.

Sure enough, the time had come; this Gulf job was one of those "favors."

Earlier that afternoon, Brinks received a phone call from one of Petruski's associates, a contact code-named "Oracle." Oracle had informed him that transmissions with an underwater research station located in the middle of the Gulf of Mexico had been lost. Then the man on the secure line gave him coordinates. Since the mission hardly seemed routine, Brinks was intrigued with the prospect of something different. He asked for details. The Oracle gave him none except to investigate, report, and clean up any potential messes. A price was not discussed; it was designated. The money was wired directly to an offshore bank account of Petruski's choosing, the sum containing more zeroes than a pitchers' duel box score. The Goon Squad was happy, but Brinks played the part of the cautious pessimist. They received no concrete details, only that there might be bodies to dispose of and wreckage to hide. Evidence to stash. The Oracle couldn't confirm anything, couldn't elaborate, couldn't answer questions, which raised several red flags in Brinks's mind. Maybe the Oracle truly didn't know. Maybe no one did. Not even Petruski himself.

This is going to be a bitch, Brinks thought as the chopper's landing skids touched down on the water. The heli gave him and the others one last bounce, lifting his ass a good six inches off the seat. Next, the pilot killed the engine and the early morning became eerily silent. Somewhere in the distant regions of his mind, Brinks still heard the whip of the propeller.

(tk-tk-tk)

(tk-tk-tk)

(tk-tk-tk)

The heli bobbed in the black expanse. The faint sound of aggravated ocean water splashing against their ride slowly overtook the silence and faded out the phantom propeller.

"Sorry about all that, y'all," the pilot said nervously, waving at them with an admission of guilt.

"Boy," Gardner said, unstrapping his buckle. "You lucky I like it rough, because if I didn't, I'd bury your head so far up your cracker ass you'd be seeing brown for a lifetime." Bellowing with laughter, Gardner stood up. The man was built like a Promethean sculpture. He strode toward the front of the chopper and popped the pilot in the right arm with a quick right hook. The pilot let out a high-pitched yelp, which oddly sounded like a squeaky chew toy getting stepped on. Gardner found this noise hilarious and erupted with more laughter, more uproarious than his previous outburst.

"Dang, Gardy!" Hanson said, slapping his knee. "I think you broke the fucker's arm!"

The pilot eyed his destroyed arm, which now lay limp at his side. "I can't move it! Fuck! I can't fucking move it!"

Gardy glanced back at his good friend with a childlike grin. "Shit! I think I did!"

They guffawed wildly.

Brinks didn't join them. He ignored the shenanigans and clicked on his Mag-Lite, searching the immediate area below. The choppy waters were littered with floating scraps of metal. For every ten pieces of building material there was one dead body. Straight down, a severed arm sailed on the uneven blanket of black water.

"What the fuck happened here?" Brinks asked no one in particular. In fact, the words weren't really meant for anyone else's ears but his own.

"Dang, that's nasty," Hanson said, viewing the lost appendage. His comment was filled with fascination rather than disgust.

The pilot vomited out his window. The regurgitation splashed across the body of the chopper.

Gardner rolled his eyes, his smile still in place. "Fucking lightweight!" The atmosphere thundered with more of the big man's laughter.

Brinks shushed him. He picked up the phone on his lap and jabbed a string digits with his finger.

"Who you calling, boss?" Hanson asked.

"The Oracle. Something seems *fucked* here."

A voice answered on one ring.

"Brinks."

"We gotta real shit show down here, O. I'm talking dead bodies every-fucking-where. This station of yours—yeah, she's surfaced. In about a million fucking pieces." He bit his lower lip and assessed their equipment, the gear stationed in the back of the chopper. The gear that was not nearly enough to complete the arduous task at hand. "Don't mean to sound all negative and shit, but it's going to take more than three men and a helicopter to clean this shit-mess up."

The Oracle paused. Then he said, "Do your best." With that simple response, he hung up.

Brinks ripped the phone away from his ear. "Motherfucker," Brinks muttered.

"What he say?" Hanson asked.

Brinks turned back to the black ocean and the floating turds that belonged to Petruski-Corp. They weren't prepared for this. Brinks figured they were here to clean something up—scoop up some dead bodies, grab a quick look of the area to make sure nothing was out of the ordinary—but not this. The entire station, or a large portion of it, had surfaced. Sure, the job paid great, but this was nuts. There was no way Petruski expected them to sweep this under the rug—or in this case, the ocean. *The son of a bitch has to know that,* Brinks thought. *Doesn't he?*

He didn't know what Petruski truly expected of them; too many man hours involved and not enough men. They didn't operate this way. Brinks didn't operate that way. *And the son of a bitch knows that,* he repeated. *He knows.*

His sixth sense tingled with confusion and skepticism. The answer to this complex puzzle seemed close, within reach, on the tip of his thoughts, only he couldn't see it, not the whole picture. Something was blinding him and when he closed his eyes to concentrate, all he saw was a check with his name on it and a long string of zeroes.

"Hanson," he finally said.

"Boss?"

Brinks pointed. "See that out there?" He pointed to the center of the wreckage. A flashing red light blinked about thirty yards away.

"Yeah, boss."

"Why don't you swim out, see what it is. Might be transmitting a distress signal. Whatever it is, bring it back. In the meantime, Gardner and I will come up with something to clear this mess. Not much dark left and I'd rather not be caught with our pants down in daylight. I don't think anyone is on patrol out here, but we can't be too sure."

"Yes, sir." Hanson swung open the helicopter door and spit a wad of chew into the darkness outside. He untethered himself from the chopper and prepared to dive. "See you fuckers in a jiff!"

They watched him jump, splash into the water, and disappear below the small black waves. Gardner followed his partner's invisible path and concentrated on the area where he predicted Hanson to resurface. About twenty seconds later, his boy materialized exactly where Gardner had set his sights on.

Brinks watched the playful expression on Gardner's face slowly melt away.

"What's the matter, soldier?" Brinks asked.

Gardner swung his head in Brinks's direction. "Something's wrong about this. Don't feel right. What you thinking, Brinks?"

Something sour filled his mouth. "I don't like it much either, soldier. But the way I see it, we can grab the explosives and blow everything to bits. That way—"

He stopped himself.

Explosives.

Why didn't he think of that before?

What if...

Brinks launched himself into a standing position and hung out the helicopter's open door, one hand gripping the metal frame, the other flapping in the air furiously. "Hanson!" he shouted as loud as he could. "Get your ass back here!" Whipping his head back toward the cockpit, he pointed at the pilot and said, "Get ready to get this bird off the ground, double-time!" He swung his attention back to Hanson and screamed at the top of his lungs, ordering him back immediately.

Jesus, this can't be fucking happening.

It was too late. Hanson had already arrived at the small blinking light. There was a brief moment when Brinks witnessed Hanson also realizing what was happening. That look of abject horror, that instant when Hanson's complexion immediately grayed, would be forever imprinted in Brinks's mind, haunting him for eternities to come.

No, God, no. Please don't end it like this.

Hanson opened his mouth to scream, but the thunderous boom of the detonation beat him to the airwaves. An explosion with the radius of a baseball diamond spat fire and smoke into the atmosphere, roiling stacks of orange and slate. The blast scattered Hanson's appendages, depositing pieces of his anatomy in various places around the exploding wreckage. Shrapnel and human gobbets rained down around them, some reaching the copter. Brinks watched a bloody chunk of Hanson smack against the cockpit window. A piece of steel followed the raw meat and cracked the glass, sending a fissure across the entire windshield.

"Noooooo!" Gardner screamed, nearly jumping into the water after his friend. The fact that Hanson was already in several pieces stopped him from going through with it. Just in case, Brinks placed his arm across his chest and shot him a cautionary glance.

"It's too late," Brinks said, the moment the pilot fired up the propellers. He turned to the idiot in the cockpit and screamed, "Get us the fuck out of here!"

Almost immediately, Brinks felt the heli lift. He ducked back into his seat and strapped himself in while thinking how easily it could have been him and not Hanson. But it wasn't him. He had sent Hanson to check the light out. He was responsible for Hanson's death. He didn't detonate the explosive, no, but it was all the same. Later he'd reconcile with this information, but for now he hammered himself with it.

He looked over at Gardner, and Gardner glared back, taking in deep breaths. He felt sorry for him. Gardner and Hanson were close, closer than Brinks was with either one of them. They often hung out with each other outside of work, and Brinks had the sneaking suspicion that the two of them were lovers. He had nothing to base this theory on except that the two of them shared an apartment, horsed around way too much, and never talked about women in the way most men talked about women. Plus, they gave each other that "look." Often. Brinks was almost certain the two of them were banging, not that he gave a shit. Brinks didn't care where they put their peckers behind closed doors; the only thing that mattered was whether the men had his back, and they had. Always. Through it all. Every time.

The sadness in Gardner's expression made Brinks's chest feel like it had split apart. An invisible hatchet settled in his breastbone. His lips quivered as he tried to work the words out. "I'm sorry, Gardy, God, I'm so fucking sor—"

What sounded like the world cracking in half erupted from below. Fire and smoke surrounded the chopper and Brinks felt his entire body drop. For a second, he thought he'd lost his stomach through his mouth. He stuck his head out the side and saw the black water below spinning, shifting wildly.

But the world below wasn't moving.

They were.

And fast.

"Fuck, fuck, fuck!" the pilot screamed. The controls before him lit up like Times Square and started making all sorts of loud tones that Brinks deemed not very fucking good.

Brinks looked down in time to witness another explosion taking shape, reaching towers of apricot and billowing smoke that merged with the black abyss above, blinding the stars. The heli rocked side to side but the pilot was able to straighten the bird out. They flew from the blast. Below, more explosives detonated, lighting up the surrounding darkness for miles in each direction.

"That was close," the pilot admitted. A nervous grin broke across his face. "For a second there, I thought we—"

A fast-paced intermittent beep interrupted his victory speech. Again, the dials and buttons on the dashboard radiated with tones of red and green. Brinks stuck his head out the chopper and looked back. The bird's tail rotor was missing, replaced a smokestack that disappeared against the onyx backdrop. Something underneath them had caught fire, too, and begun to sizzle and spark.

His stomach swirled along with their ride.

The pilot continued to bark long strings of obscenities while he mashed every button on the menu, turned every dial. Gardner yelled something from the back, something about abandoning ship, but Brinks barely heard him. He closed his eyes and watched the best moments of his life play out before him.

As the chopper spun errantly, plummeting toward the black ocean below, he thought if Petruski wanted him dead then the bastard was going to have to try harder. A lot harder. He wasn't going down easily. Not like this.

Sudden darkness powered off his thoughts as the bird collapsed on the obsidian expanse. Brinks barely felt a thing before a black wave clapped over him, diluting his consciousness.

7.

About a hundred miles south of the western coast of Florida sits Key Water Island, a small, secluded private island en route to Mexico. The land is no more sixty square miles and its inhabitants are mostly tropical greenery and indigenous birds. Half the island is used as a small fishing port, which sees no more than about a hundred people at one time. A small hotel rests on the eastern side of the island, run and maintained by the Rudder family who call Key Water Island home twenty-four-seven, three-sixty-five. Other than those constants, the island is consistently in a state of flux in terms of population. Fishermen who venture out this far enjoy the quietness and seclusion Key Water Island provides. There's only one restaurant and watering hole for them to choose from, located inside the Rudders' hotel, but not a single patron has ever complained about the quality of food or service; the grub is always tasty and the beer is always chilled, both served with a smile.

Key Water Island has a rich, albeit muddled history. Most notably, the pirate Blackbeard was said to have used Key Water as a place of refuge, a secret getaway complete with underground tunnels, deadly booby traps, and lost artifacts. Some historians refute this claim, saying the infamous buccaneer never traveled that far north. Others claim the Blackbeard rumors completely true, insisting he used the island frequently while fleeing the clutches of his many adversaries. With this came rumors of buried treasure and for a long while there were charters arranged to invade Key Water Island in search of said loot. However, no one ever found so much as a penny, and soon after Key Water Island was forgotten about until the Rudder family claimed the unmarked land as their own sometime during the twentieth century.

In 1963, the marine biology department of Florida State convinced the university to purchase a small plot of land from the Rudders, opposite the hotel side of the island. Upon the transaction, they built a small, ocean-facing villa, equipped with a fully functioning laboratory stocked with state-of-the-art technology and all the supplies the department could afford, which at the time was plentiful. Back then the head professors held a keen interest in the growing population of bull sharks and the small gathering of Great Whites just off Key Water's coast. Every year during the first week of September, hundreds of bull sharks congregated to feed off the local supply of fish. Great Whites made rare appearances at the annual feeding frenzy. Because of this, the university thought it was the best chance they had to study these magnificent creatures up close and personal without having to travel a great distance at great cost. They thought it'd be great for the students and great for the university. And it was. The seasonal excursion became a staple in Florida State's biology department's curriculum. Every year, the head professor would escort a few hand-selected students to the island. Those with the best academic qualities were chosen. The school never missed a trip. Never. Not once.

Sharkwater Beach was always
(and forever would be)
tradition.

* * *

Jill tossed her duffel bag on the bed. She collapsed down next to it. Closing her eyes, an uneasy warmth settled in her brain. Although it only just happened, she tried to remember how she ended up here, this familiar predicament. At this place. A place of many memories, most of which she was fond of, except for one—the image repeating itself in her mind—that burned her chest in a way that convinced her she was having a heart attack.

She took a deep breath, then blew the spent oxygen out her nose.

Panic attack more likely, she thought, concentrating on regulating the air to her lungs.

Knuckles rapping on the door frame.

The door to her room was open so the uninvited guest crossed the threshold cautiously, tip-toeing and peeking around the corner of the small foyer. "Jill?"

Her eyes shot open. "Yes?"

She found Pickard leaning against the wall like he was posing for some 80s pop-rock album cover. He wore a navy blue windbreaker and white shorts that failed to cover his knees. It made him look more like a track and field coach than the marine biology department head, but Jill didn't mention it. She thought opening her mouth to speak was an invitation for vomit.

"You okay?" he asked.

She nodded and clutched the pillow next to her. "Yeah," she moaned. "Feeling a little seasick."

His confusion resulted in a simultaneous frown and wink. "You're a bad liar. A hundred charters we've taken together and never once saw you green. You've never been seasick a day in your life, I'd wager."

She jerked her shoulders. "Maybe it's something I ate."

Pickard looked like he wanted speak, tell her he hadn't seen her eat a thing all morning, but for the moment he kept his lips sealed. "Listen. We're heading down to the beach. Come hang out for a bit." It sounded like a question. "We'll scope out some good spots. My students are getting the equipment ready, although, surprisingly the bull sharks haven't arrived yet. Thought they might be here by now, but... you know. Whatever's out there might be affecting the neighborhood patterns."

Jill nodded. "Sounds like a blast," she said perfunctorily. She rose from the mattress like a ghoul, dead-like. Her brain felt as if someone had used it as a gong. "Got any aspirin?"

"I think one of my students might."

"Great."

"Sure you're okay? Not acting like the Jill I know."

The Jill you know is dead, motherfucker. You killed her. Remember?

Instead of speaking her mind, she faked a smile and pushed herself to her feet. "Ask me again and I'll use you as shark bait. I'm fine. Get over it."

Pickard raised his hands to his ears, a gesture of surrender. "Okay. Relax. Just making sure. No need to get all Lizzie Borden on me." He turned for the exit.

"Neil?" she asked, squinting as if the lights were too much on her eyes, although they weren't even on, the room still crawling with daytime shadows.

"Yeah, what's up?"

"The first crazy thing we see—you have to call the mainland. Promise me? No bullshit. We call the coast guard and get the hell out of here."

A certain look occupied his face and Jill knew he wanted to rant on about non-territorial waters and private islands and how no one might even come to help them if they did find themselves in a precarious situation. How the only law out here was the one the Rudders upheld. The family employed a small security squad, comprised of ex-United States military. They were paid to ensure no one took advantage of the lawless boundaries. After all, pirates still existed. They just didn't have cool names like Blackbeard and Calico Jack, nor did they sport lavishly detailed headwear and sail elegant wooden vessels.

Instead of explaining this, he said, "Yeah, I promise."

She nodded even though she knew he was lying. The man never did have much of a poker face. She read him like the Sunday funnies.

After he disappeared from the room, she shuffled to the bathroom where she washed her face in the sink, toweled off, and stared at her sad reflection in the mirror. As she silently questioned herself about the real reason she agreed to this impromptu adventure, she noticed new wrinkles in her flesh that hadn't been there a few days ago. Had seeing Neil again stressed her out that much? To the point where her skin was sagging? Was such a thing even possible?

She rubbed her tired eyes and gave herself a second look. She didn't look like the fatigued old hag she had moments ago. Her eyes and brain were playing tricks on her. Her flesh was no more wrinkled than it was yesterday.

Done with abusing her image, she headed outside. Her room was on the second floor of the villa and faced a picturesque view of the ocean, cinematic in its scope. The sand was almond and had been soft under her bare feet, although much too hot for her to enjoy sinking her toes in. The waters were teal near the shoreline, almost crystalline, a quality lost the farther out her eyes traveled. Beyond the ocean was a midnight blue, dark and unwelcoming. The dock where they had parked their charter had been painted driftwood gray, now peeling with time and careless maintenance. It extended a good thirty feet into the ocean, plenty of room for other boats, not there would be any. Clusters of palms and other tropical shrubbery flanked the villa, keeping their quarters secluded from any neighbors, even though Pickard informed them that no one from the Rudders' side of the island ever came over. They were all alone out here.

Just like old times, she thought.

She strolled down the balcony and made her way over to the stairs, using the railing for balance. She wasn't lying to Pickard; she really felt ill. Maybe not seasick, but something. Her head ached. Her neck went painfully stiff. Her stomach knotted like a discarded roll of 35mm. Sharp cramps radiated through her midsection, feeling like she had been stabbed over and over again by hundreds of boiled blades. Plain and simple, Jill McCourty was a hot mess.

She made her way down the stairs, taking each step slowly as if they were dodging her feet. Once down, sandals planted on the cracked concrete patio, she hunched over and placed her hands on her knees. She had kept her body in good shape over the years, hitting the gym regularly and swimming at the Y for an hour each day, at least five times a week. She had passed every physical exam the sheriff's department threw at her. In her mind, she was in peak physical condition. No ailments whatsoever.

But something *was* wrong with her. She couldn't remember ever feeling this way, so weak, so…

Stressed.

A panic attack? It was the only logical explanation. The world around her seemed brighter and spun slowly. Her nerves tingled throughout her body, pins and needles raging in her arms and legs. Her heart changed directions like a school of frantic fish.

"Hey there!" shouted a chipper voice, nearly causing Jill's head to explode.

Her entire body jerked. "Jesus! You scared the shit out of me."

A bouncy girl with beach-blond pigtails stood before her. She wore a sleeveless FSU T-shirt, a size too big so that it covered her bikini bottom, giving off the illusion that she was bottomless. She had the figure of a flagpole and the charm of a Costbusters' greeter. Her stretching smile was enough to make Jill barf. She swallowed back bile.

"Sorry, Jill," the girl said happily. "Didn't mean to!"

Jill cracked a forced smile and waved off her jubilant concern. "Don't sweat it…" She snapped her fingers several times, trying to recall the girl's name.

"Ally."

"Ally. Sorry. I'm terrible with names." Jill surveyed the beach. "Where's the professor?"

"Professor Pickard?"

"There another professor on this island I don't know about?"

Ally slapped her forehead. "Duh. Yeah, I think he went to grab a soda or something. Not sure. The rest of us are setting up the equipment down near the shore. You wanna come?"

There was something likable about Ally despite her sharing a personality with every cheerleader Jill went to high school with. She forced herself to hate the girl. It was probably because of how soon her thoughts turned on her. For some reason, Jill couldn't buy into that Ally was one of Pickard's top students. Nope. She assumed that the girl was here because Pickard was giving her some extra credit. And by extra credit, she of course meant—

(Pickard and Ally crawling under the sheets. They're already undressed. Breathing heavily. She sucks on his neck. He coos like he does when he senses something he likes. She moves down his body. Down.

Down.

Down.)

—the two were sleeping together. She remembered Pickard had the sexual appetite of a jackrabbit and the projected images in her brain caused shivers to cascade down her spine. Nausea was summoned and it took everything Jill had to prevent herself from going Linda Blair all over the place.

"You okay?" a small voice asked.

"Hm?" Jill asked, not realizing how hard she was biting her lip. A coppery flavor ran over her tongue.

"Are you okay?" Ally repeated. "You look off."

"Thanks for noticing, but I'll be swell." She started walking toward the shoreline.

Ally trotted after her. "Professor Pickard told us you were his best student."

Those damn images again. This time, Jill was the one beneath the sheets sucking on his neck candy.

"Yeah, well. I was okay. I guess."

"Don't be so modest." A cherubic giggle followed the advice. "What were you most interested in?" When it looked like Jill wasn't going to answer, she said, "I love oceanography."

Jill spun around like a top. "Listen, Ally. You seem like a swell girl. But really. Please don't be so… so… so *you*. You know what I mean?"

"I… don't—um, what?"

"Let's start with your voice. It's annoying. And I hate it."

"Oh. Okay." The girl looked gut shot. Her eyes wandered toward the bent palms on her left. Her smile died off instantly. "I can, you know, leave you alone."

"That would be amazing."

"I was just trying to be nice," she said, her words lacking enthusiasm of the smallest degree.

Jill took a deep breath and collected her senses. "Yeah, I know. I get it. Just… *dammit.* I'm having a rough go of it lately. Mind giving me a break?"

Ally nodded.

"Sorry I yelled at you, Ally. I didn't mean to. I'm… I'm such a twat." She paused, expecting Ally to agree, but the eighteen-year-old kept quiet and still, either waiting for more apologies or the awkwardness of their conversation to end. She would have preferred to be cussed out. "Let's go down to the shore. See what the others are up to. Okay?"

"Okay," Ally said. Her positive energy returned, but not as vibrant as before. "Follow me."

Jill trailed her to the shoreline, hoping their mystery shark would reveal itself soon so she could head back home and resume her normal life. Escape the past, this island, and the memories that plagued her here.

Later she'd wish the shark hadn't come at all.

8.

Blinking open his eyes, he felt warm water rush up his throat and explode out his mouth. He forced himself over on his side, letting the rest of the saltwater drain onto the sand below. The hoarse croak of his lungs struggling for air sounded a lot like a clogged vacuum hose. Completely drained, he lay there for a while until a wave of energy washed over him. When he felt well enough, he pulled himself to a seated position and surveyed the damage to his body, which was surprisingly minimal. His pants were ripped in multiple places, white ribbons of shredded denim. His arms and hands were cut as if he had skidded across a parking lot full of broken glass. The wounds were almost closed, the dark maroon slashes crusted over. The sliced flesh burned from the saltwater, nothing he couldn't deal with. The worst pain came from the blistery burns that riddled his arms. Heat pelted his face, feeling like he had been scalded by a bucket of boiling water, which got him wondering how long he'd been exposed to the blazing sun.

But those thoughts quickly faded when he looked up and saw two men garbed in full black looking down at him. Armed with automatic weapons and rugged appearances, they didn't look like the kind of people who would rescue him.

"Who are you and where are we?" the bald white dude with a chin-strap beard asked. He was the smaller of the two, but both men were equally built like cage fighters.

"My name is Chris," CJ said. It was difficult to speak. His throat was so dry the words felt like they clawed their way out. As soon as he thought the worst was over, a sudden rush of something hot climbed his throat and he spewed out another volcanic stream of water. The purge felt good, better than those before it, and he was confident that was the last of it. "Friends call me CJ." It wasn't easy to breathe but it was getting better. Short breaths soon became long ones, and in a few minutes the air flow regulated.

"And where exactly are we, CJ?" the tall black man asked. His tone demanded facts. Nostrils flaring, the man pursed his lips.

Sweat poured down his forehead as if it were raining. "Do you have any idea?"

CJ took in surroundings. Before him lay an endless body of tropical water. Looking down, he found himself sitting on a soft bed of pale sand. Granules had stuck to the sweaty parts of him, the back of his arms and legs. Behind him, a limitless row of beach grass stood like an invading army sent to protect the paradisiacal forest behind it. An assortment of palms, cacti, hibiscus, banana and mango trees, and Buttonwoods towered, leaving little or no room between them for travel.

CJ returned his attention to the two men. "I have no idea."

The response didn't sit well with either of them.

"No idea, huh?" the tall black man asked. "That's great. That's just fucking great."

"Calm down, Gardy. We don't—"

The man called Gardy slammed his gun on the ground. "I'm not going to calm down!" he roared. CJ flinched. The man's eyes expanded to twice their usual size. "Hanson is dead, Brinks! Fucking dead! That motherfucker Petruski set us up! He set us up!"

The other man—Brinks—grabbed his friend by the collar and hoisted the taller man off the ground a good three inches. CJ was impressed with the man's strength.

"Get a hold of yourself, Gardner!"

"Fuck you, Brinks!"

"No, fuck you!"

While the two men grappled with each other and yelled obscenities, CJ found himself entranced by the tranquil waters, getting lost in the gentle waves that collapsed on the shoreline. It was then he remembered what was stalking these calm waters, the terror that came from beneath the surface.

His memory came back to him.

Bodies. Bobbing on the surface. Face down. Blood fogging the water. Exploding burgundy clouds.

He thought of his friend Duke, his fishing partner, their last ride out on the Gulf—*teeth, lots of teeth. The size of a dinner plate. Chomping down. Breaking bones. Duke screaming. His mouth filling with saltwater and blood. Sinking. Deeper into the abyss. Deeper into the black. Deeper into hell*—the wind at their backs. A new life. No longer slaves to Big Tom and all of his seedy bullshit. Freedom, the kind they both needed. He'd miss Duke's smile, his goofy persona, his semi-terrible jokes, being the test audience for his new material, his unique charm.

Duke is two now. Severed below his abdomen. An upper and lower half, although one could hardly tell which is which. His innards float like lifeless jellyfish now, enshrouded in a copper cloud of death. His eyes are open. His mouth moves like a fish. Open. Close. Open again. Closed forever. There's nothing left of him when the gigantic predator closes in for seconds, taking his head between its jaws and biting down, flatting his cranium like a tractor-trailer wheel running over a watermelon. He's gone forever behind an unfurling blood storm of murky nothingness.

Damn, he'll miss his friend. The sentimental memories and the vicious visions of his brutal demise instigate tears, a steady stream pumping from the corners of his eyes.

The two men were finished with their argument by the time the water works started.

"Fuck is wrong with you?" Gardner asked.

Between sobs, CJ managed to croak, "Duke..."

The two soldiers exchanged glances.

"Son," Brinks said, kneeling down. "Do you know how long you've been out there?"

CJ shook his head, unable to comprehend how he'd survived the shark attack and not drown in the Gulf. A small part of him remembered entering the beast's mouth and having his bones crushed between its massive jaws. *Maybe that did happen.* Maybe the shark did obliterate him and this was hell. He had always pictured the underworld as a deserted island with no sunscreen. The blisters on his flesh were almost proof enough.

"From the looks of those sun blisters," Brinks said, kneeling down before him and examining his arms, "I'd say a day. Maybe two. You might have sun poisoning. God willing, it hasn't entered your bloodstream. But you're in bad shape, kid, and if we don't find you a doctor or some antibiotics soon—well, I'm afraid the infection will only get worse. I guess you know what that means."

CJ looked at the dried vomit on his shirt and agreed with him.

He *felt* poisoned. Dizzy. Disoriented. Hell, a second ago he thought he was dead and this was the afterlife. He could almost feel the infection coursing through his veins, pervading his body, affecting his vital organs. How long did he have before his system shut down?

Brinks was right. He needed a doctor or medicine fast.

Pushing thoughts of his demise aside, he concentrated on the sprawling indigo liquid before him. "There's something out there."

Brinks and Gardner eyed him suspiciously, awaiting clarification.

"Something big."

Gardner chewed the side of his mouth. "Care to elaborate?"

"A shark." He pictured that dorsal fin, that obsidian sail. It was like no shark he'd ever seen before. At first he thought it was a killer whale, but no. It was all shark. A big shark. Blacker than the night sky. "Only... bigger. Black."

"A big black shark?" Gardner asked. "Was it an orca? Heard there's a ton of them out here."

"Wasn't an orca. I've seen orca. This was..." He swallowed what felt like knives. "Shit, I can't even describe it. It's like it wasn't real. Something out of a goddamn nightmare."

"Okay then, Mr. Mysterious," Brinks said, rising to his feet and extending CJ his right hand. "Can you stand?"

"Maybe. My legs are bad to begin with."

With the two soldiers' help, CJ managed. His whole body ached but his legs were the worst. The muscles burned, injecting him with pain and discomfort all the way down to the bone.

"Let's get under the shade," Brinks said, nodding to the tropical copse ahead of him. "We'll get our bearings, find out exactly where the fuck we are, and figure out a way home."

Gardner added, "And find Petruski. Break that motherfucker's neck."

"That too, buddy." CJ noticed the glossy sheen in the tough man's eyes. "That too."

9.

The young man sporting dreadlocks and a pink bandana tapped the sides of the faux sea lion, then raised his hands in the air as if he had just navigated through the complexities of the Callan-Symanzik equation. He stood over his completed task with a "I just smoked too much" smile and "positive vibes, man" swagger. The rubber shell that would only pass as genuine to dimwitted underwater predators looked nothing more than cheap prosthetics to the rest of them, particularly Jill. She recalled the quality of their decoys five years ago being much better. More realistic. Unimpressed, she looked down at the sad-looking hollow creature with a hand over mouth, hiding her yawn.

"Voila!" Evan Ballard shouted, unable to rid his face of his proud grin. "Came out better than I thought!"

Jill coughed into her hand. "Sharks fall for that, huh?"

Evan lost half of his smile. "Of course. Worked well last year. Strapped a GoPro right to it. Beats using a real sea lion. Less expensive to replace, too. You know. In case…" He made jaws with his arms and clapped his hands together. "When they do get caught, sharks usually tell pretty quickly that they aren't real. If the damage is minimal, we can repair them. Sometimes they get overzealous and rip them up."

"Noice," Jill said with enough sarcasm even the stoner picked up on it. She couldn't tell if Pickard's students knew everything she said was dripping with derision, but she no longer cared. If her not wanting to be there wasn't already obvious, it soon would be. The more time passed, the more she realized she shouldn't have come. Of all the dumb decisions she'd made over the last few years, this was up there with the best of them.

"Last year's students were able to grab some high-quality footage," said the brunette with faded freckles on her cheeks. The girl who had introduced herself as Monica back on the boat now hovered over Jill's right shoulder. "In fact, some people from Discovery were interested in purchasing some of it for B-roll."

"Special," Jill quipped. "So when do we push this pup in the water?"

Evan shrugged. "We were going to wait for Professor Pickard to finish his phone call."

Jill scanned the shoreline, then peeked back at the villa over her left shoulder. Pickard was nowhere. "Where is that scoundrel?"

"I think he's on the phone with his wife," Monica said.

Jill's stomach plummeted into her toes. "His what now?" Her astonishment brought uneasy glances from the crew.

Monica shifted her eyes between Jill and the other students. "His wife," she said, as if this were common knowledge the whole world knew, like the name of the first man on the moon or who won last year's Super Bowl.

"Oh. Right. Her." Jill swallowed what felt like a fist.

Ally furrowed her brow. "You don't know Professor Bowman? Annabelle?"

"Oh yeah!" Jill said, trying to play it off as something she had simply forgotten. "I know her. Well, not really. I know of her. That counts, right?" She felt her pores open and ooze beads of sweat. She wondered if the others could smell the lies as they rolled awkwardly off her tongue. "How long have they been married again?" She knew it was a suspicious question, but at this point who cared? She couldn't believe Neil had omitted this important piece of information. And now that she thought about it, she didn't remember seeing a wedding band. And she would have. *Oh, that rotten son of a bitch.* In that moment, *she* felt like the dirty one and wondered how the wife would feel if she knew about her, knew that she had joined her husband on this little excursion, spending an undetermined amount of time at a place where they once fucked, and fucked a lot. *Stupid, stupid, stupid.*

"Two years, I think," Ally said, as if she were asking a question, not answering one. "Maybe longer."

"Oh right." Jill knocked her forehead with the heel of her palm. "I knew that." The world around her began to twist and whirl, as if some cosmic vacuum cleaner were sucking up reality right before her eyes. "Would you three excuse me for a minute? I'm still feeling a little queasy from the boat. I need to lie down before I fall down."

Legitimately concerned, Evan asked, "Want me to walk you

back to your room?"

She raised her hand. "No, thank you. I can handle it."

As she stormed her way back to the villa, she spotted Neil on the balcony, pacing back and forth, waving his hand out in front of him, explaining something to someone via his iPhone. He didn't look particularly happy, which rejuvenated some—although not hardly enough—of Jill's sullen mood. She marched up the stairs, a sudden pain infiltrating her chest, spreading down her arms and into her fingertips. Pins and needles burglarized her nervous system. She thought her body was failing her, then she realized she was, in fact, experiencing a panic attack.

"No, Belle. Listen to me," Pickard went on. Now he was flapping his hand with heated frustration, pantomiming the further explanation of whatever point he was trying to make. "I didn't tell you because I knew *this* was how you'd react." He perked up when he spotted Jill's presence. His expression went slack. "Because I know you," he continued. "Okay, fine. Agree to disagree." He stared into Jill's eyes like maybe she had done something wrong. "Okay, I have to go. We'll chat later."

He slipped the phone in his pocket, then folded his arms across his chest and leaned back on his heels.

"So…" he said.

"So? *So?* That's all you have to say for yourself?" She didn't give him a chance to explain. "You're fucking married?"

He pushed his arms out as if to say *so what?*

"You didn't think that was information I would have liked to know?"

"I don't see what that has to do with our academic research."

Her face resembled a bear spotting a territorial trespasser. "You lied to me."

Insulted, he shook a finger at her. "I never lied to you."

"No, you just never told me you were married. Same as lying in my book."

"Well, I don't like your book very much. I think your book sucks." He said this very matter-of-factly, and she wanted to rip his throat out. "Jill, my personal life doesn't matter. What matters is what we discovered. Or rather, what we *uncovered*. That's what's important here. That's what we need to focus on. The past, my personal relationships—all of that pales in comparison to this." With his finger, he directed her attention out at sea.

She shook her head. "You're unbelievable. At least tell me what you two were arguing about."

Frustration boiling over, he rolled his eyes and turned his body. "I just said none of that matters. It's none of your business."

"You told her I was here, didn't you?"

No answer.

That's a big you-bet-your-sweet-ass-I-did.

She threw her head back and moaned. "Goddammit, Neil. Why didn't you just tell me?"

Rotating back to her, he opened his mouth and placed his hands on his hips. "Because," he said with a short breath. "I knew you wouldn't have come."

She hadn't given that much thought, but it still wasn't an excuse. On the other hand, it would have been nice to have kept that personal day.

"Neil, I have no idea how to trust you." She bit her lip. "Time and time again, you've proven to be the sleaziest sack of shit I know."

He didn't argue.

"I think I should go. Like back home. Make the arrangements?"

Pickard's eyes fluttered with disbelief. "Jill, no—"

"Please?" A disgusted look from head to toe. She brushed it off best she could. "Least you could do for breaking a girl's heart once upon a time ago."

Avoiding eye contact with her, he huffed and said, "Okay, fine. Whatever you want. I'll have someone come get you."

"Thank you." She turned. "I'll be in my room. It might be better if we never speak again."

Pickard opened his mouth to plead with her, but her gait suggested she was done talking and wouldn't turn around even if she were heading into the crimson-crusted maw of a bloodthirsty sea beast.

10.

The Ocean Queen glided through the murky deep, following the vibrations coming from nearby lifeforms. The idea of coming to land had become so strong that she couldn't get it out of her football-sized brain. Although she had no knowledge of the watery world in which she now existed, she did her best to keep a constant pace, cruising along, hoping to reach land before the birth of her young. A small worry came over her: how was she to give birth on land? She didn't have lungs. No legs. No pre-existing concept of a terrestrial existence. Aquatic survival was all she'd known. Even under the supervision of the humans she existed in the deep, albeit an area barely big enough to contain her lengthy and bulbous form.

More worrisome thoughts populated: like, how—if she'd never seen land—did she know such a place existed? Surely the idea came from somewhere. Hadn't it? These thoughts concerned her, but her brain had become a nervous octopus and the thought-provoking musings spilled out of her like black, poisonous ink. She wondered weird things like how old she was and became confused how she understood the concept of time. How she correlated time with existence was a subject seemingly beyond her comprehension. Also, her basic instincts told her she was shark, but she couldn't decipher how she knew what a shark was, or how she became one.

How she became the biggest to ever live.

The Ocean Queen.

She weighed those troublesome tidbits of trivia. How did she know so much about the world, all of its intricacies, all of its devilish details, if the only thing she had experienced was what the humans allowed her to?

The humans.

They did things to her. They were responsible for this.

She recalled being poked and prodded while under their confinement. Pain. Tours of agony that funneled through her body, extending from her bullet-shaped nose down to the tip of her caudal fin. It was a torturous experience, sessions upon sessions of intense suffering. But for some reason, the more she thought about it, the more that wasn't completely true.

The more she explored her past and navigated through her memories, the more she thought she had come from somewhere else and landed in the humans' clutches by mere unfortunate luck. The humans didn't give birth to her; she was not their creation. That right belonged to another, perhaps some faceless omnipotence. She hadn't been created. Her form originated from somewhere else, somewhere far from the cerulean world she now occupied. A world where water sources were scarce and drying out. A place where land was abundant. Not green and luxuriant like the one she currently sought, but a land where gleaming, obsidian rocks stood like towers, scraping against forlorn skies. The overarching formations twinkled under the birth of ten moons. Worm-like creatures dragged their shriveled, depleted bodies across the colorless soil, in search of fresh water supplies. The dry, chalky world fed on them, and soon the many moons would die, bringing forth the sun that would bake them into oblivion.

She didn't understand how she knew these things, conjured these images in her mind as clear as she could see the small, innocent seal swimming across her nose. The slippery bag of meat jagged through the water, cutting back and forth with unbelievable speed. The creature was small and agile and the Ocean Queen noticed something alien strapped to its back, a structure of some sort. It looked oddly human, or rather—something manufactured by human hand, a tool of sorts. Perhaps utilized for destruction. That's all she associated with humans. Destruction and suffering, agony and devilry.

She raced after the creature as it bounced through the deep blue.

Toward the shores of an alien world.

Her babies rolled in her stomach, eagerly awaiting the new epoch of food chain dominance.

11.

They had each taken an arm and scooted CJ through the tropical jungle, exhausting every ounce of strength they had in the tank. The kid's leg was in worse shape than the rest of him. The slightest amount of pressure caused him to gasp. He was a tough kid, at least Brinks thought so. He didn't want to show how much it hurt, but his reaction to the pain was natural. Even if he'd been able to walk under his own power, the sun poisoning would have delayed him, slowing the group down. They made do with their tripod approach.

After pushing through the palms and other exotic shrubbery, they came to an open portion of the island, free of overhead foliage. A heat-laden breeze gusted off the coast, brushing against their faces and spotting their flesh with flecks of saltwater. The wind soothed, a temporary refreshment. The men knew the moment wouldn't last and stopped to take in the brief reprieve.

It was Brinks who first and made out the small mansion in the distance, resting on the apex of a craggy cliff overlooking the Gulf. It stood four-stories high and Brinks counted ten windows on each floor. Details emerged as they walked ahead and closed the distance. The painted-white exterior had begun to peel, a battle lost to inclement weather and the disposition of time. Navy blue shutters accompanied every window, and he could see only one was slightly askew. There were no cars or helicopters parked in the long stretch of land opposite the crag, but there were about a dozen fishing charters docked at the base of the cliff. Bouts of rough waves knocked them around and Brinks knew from the agitated waters that a storm was headed their way.

The group was just far enough away that no one could make out the lettering across the face of the mansion, but regardless of what it said, they knew what they had found.

Refuge.

The three of them retired from the shade provided by the jungle's leafy canopy. As one unit they hobbled along, reaching the outskirts of the mansion's property. The climb to the top of the hill proved difficult, but they managed. CJ and his badly battered body held them back. At one point, Brinks contemplated scooping the kid up and carrying him up the incline. But the kid persevered, pushed through it, fought off the pain and the poison coursing through his veins.

The lettering read "Rudders'," which gave no inclination to what the place was—a hotel, a restaurant, or someone's personal vacation spot. Brinks figured the latter wouldn't warrant a big sign out front, spelled out in bold, wine-red letters. He placed his bet on the first two guesses.

As they neared, Brinks found them a nice little spot in the shade provided by the tall building. A place where they could gather their senses, figure out what to do next. They planted CJ on the ground, allowing him to rest his back on the concrete walkway. The kid looked glad to be out of the sun. He covered his face with his palms, perhaps to hide tears. Brinks saw how tough the kid was and how he'd kept from crying throughout the entire journey. But everyone had their breaking point, and it appeared the kid had reached his.

"What's the play?" Gardner asked, dropping to one knee.

Brinks looked the place over. It seemed to have been maintained for the most part. The fascia was all new composite and the gutters were sparkling white, recently replaced. The paint on the Texture 1-11 siding had peeled and bubbled in places, but the pallet full of five-gallon containers stationed by a nearby maintenance shed suggested that that was next on the to-do list.

Brinks turned to Gardner and said, "Place is obviously in use. A hotel, my guess."

Gardner nodded. "Yeah. Bar, too. Saw a sign for drink specials. Two-dollar Tropical Sunrises." A smile broke across his face. Brinks was glad to see the loss of his friend hadn't altered his mood too much. "Don't know what the fuck that is, but it sounds delish."

Brinks raised his bushy eyebrows. "Must have missed that sign. Doesn't surprise me that you didn't."

"What are you trying to say, boss?"

"That you're a fucking lush."

Gardner dwelled on this information for a few seconds, then nodded vigorously. "Yeah, okay. You got me there."

What sounded like a bad air leak interrupted their conversation. *"Water."*

They glanced down at CJ. His lips were cracked. His skin had taken on the hue of a boiled crab. Blisters had opened on his flesh, raw and oozing with thick pus.

Gardner inhaled a breath. "Kid's in a world of hurt."

"Well, shit. He's not exactly our number one priority."

Gardner didn't exactly disagree. "You want to leave him, say the word. But we didn't just lug his ass through the jungle to leave him to die. Did we?"

Brinks tried to remember why they had brought the kid with them in the first place. *Because it was the right thing to do.* He wasn't sure whose voice that was, but he didn't like it. It sounded too much like his own. "No, we didn't." It would have been easier to leave the kid behind, let the sun have him. But Brinks couldn't do it. He figured watching Hanson burst into pieces had something to do with it. His friend's death was fucking with his conscious. "Bringing him indoors would be ideal."

"Can't exactly waltz into the place with our weapons and a dying kid, could we? Fuck, for all we know, a bunch of island rednecks could be in there, each with a gun of their own. Judging from the boats on the dock, there seems to be a bunch of them. You don't want to mess with island rednecks."

"I don't think *island rednecks* is a thing," Brinks said, almost smiling.

"Bet your honky ass it's a thing." Gardner nodded toward the front of the mansion. "Go ahead. You go in there with your gun out and see what happens. I'll count the bullets in you when you come back out."

Brinks pinched his lips together, then slipped the strap of his gun over his head, setting the weapon down next to CJ. "All right. I'll go in unarmed. I'll see what's what, and I'll at least bring back some water."

"Bring me two."

"Noted."

Brinks crouched and made his way around the hotel. Scurrying down the walkway, he located the front entrance door. Standing before it, he stiffened up, straightened his back and cracked his knuckles. Then he stretched his neck until made a satisfying popping noise, like a wine cork shooting off. Taking a deep breath, he pushed through the entrance and stepped inside the bar.

Several heads turned toward his entry. As he glanced around the room, he felt like a dangerous gunslinger entering a foreign saloon in those old spaghetti westerns. He stepped forward, directing himself to the bar. The sound of his boots tapping the old wooden planks was the only noise heard. He realized how weird he looked walking in here, decked out in all-black military fatigues, his flesh peppered with cuts and bruises. There were probably twenty fishermen occupying the bar and lounge area, every single one of them turned and facing him.

There wasn't enough booze in the world to kill the stench of gutted fish and saltwater. Brinks tried to keep himself from gagging.

The bartender serving a big foamy brew to a local patron winked at Brinks, then asked, "Help you, friend?" He had a Southern twang to his accent that was almost homey.

Island rednecks, Brinks thought, unable to contain the small smile from occupying his face.

"Looking for a phone," he said casually.

At first, the bartender only stared at him, refusing to deviate his gaze. After shutting his till, he stretched his arm and pointed to the far corner of the bar. "Payphone back there."

"Don't have any money." He winked at the man with long, raven-black hair. "This seems like a friendly place. Was hoping you could do me a solid and spare me some change."

Another cold gaze that seemed practically endless. "Okay," he said, finding his grin. He reached into the tip jar and came out with a fistful of quarters. He dropped the change into Brinks's open palm. "Call is on me, stranger."

Brinks nodded, thanking the man for his generosity. "I appreciate the hell out of that."

He turned and headed for the small cubby in the back corner of the room. He felt the bartender's gaze follow him to the phone, but most of the other patrons had resumed their conversations about women, fish, and their routine sea adventures.

Once in the cubby, Brinks leaned against the wall. He picked up the phone and put it against his ear. Dropped the coins in the slot. Punched the memorized digits. Listened to the tonal ring. Third beep, a groggy, in-no-mood-for-shit sounding voice answered. "Hello?"

"You motherfucker," Brinks said in a low voice. There was a table no more than ten feet away and he didn't want the three burly fishermen hearing a word of his business. Feeling somewhat safe inside the bar and free from an attack of any kind, he turned and faced the wall, concealing his conversation from the rest of the room. "Did you know?"

"Brinks?"

"No, motherfuckin' Charlie Bronson." Brinks spat. "Of course it's Brinks, you asshole."

The man on the other end sounded out of breath. "Shit, what are you doing calling me?"

"Don't give me that shit, Ronald. Like you don't fucking know."

"Brinks, I swear to Christ's left testicle, I have no idea what you're talking about." Brinks heard the flick of a lighter coming to life. The burning of paper and sizzling of tobacco quickly followed. The man exhaled into the phone, creating static in Brinks's ear. "But you calling me, can't be fucking good."

"Our mutual friend, Nikolai Petruski, tried to have us killed this morning."

Silence. Then: "You? The Goon Squad? Really. That's interesting."

"Is it? Is it interesting? You know, if I didn't know any better, Ronald, I'd say you're a little fucking surprised to hear my voice. Somewhat disappointed, too."

Ronald blew into his ear again. "Fuck, Brinks. You know it ain't like that."

"Ron. Hanson is dead, Gardner and I were almost blown to smithereens. Tell me what the hell is going on. And you better tell me quick, you slimy son of a bitch, or I'll find you, Ron. I'll find you and I'll fucking hurt you."

Another long sigh, and Brinks couldn't tell if he was expelling another plume of smoke, or readying himself to expose important information. Brinks hoped the latter.

"All right, listen. I didn't find out until late last night, but yes, I knew about the burn."

Brinks felt his muscles tighten and a fire rage beneath his skin.

"I'm sorry. It's just business. That's all it is. Even if I wanted to warn you, it would've been too late. Had I sent you a clue, I'd be as dead you three right now."

"Big mistake, Ronny. Big goddamn mistake."

"Fuck you, Brinks. You had to know it was coming. Too much of a liability and Petruski gets nervous easily. I warned you not to trust him."

"I trusted you, shit-sack. We *all* trusted you." In the reflection cast by the metal pay phone box, Brinks saw the veins in his forehead popping. "Hanson died because you're a coward."

"Well, guess I can live with that." The bastard coughed. "Want my advice? Wherever you are, stay there. The quicker Petruski finds out you aren't dead, the quicker he'll have that rectified."

"I'm on some island in the middle of nowhere. Probably ten, fifteen miles from site X."

"Uh-huh," Ronald said, seeming uninterested.

"Was hoping you could send a chopper. Pick us up. Make up for your betrayal."

"Don't think that'll happen, bud. Best hang tight. Relax." His voice suddenly changed, becoming less of the hum-drum robot he'd been. "Say, you see anything... peculiar out there? At site X, I mean."

"You mean besides enough debris to fill a scrap yard, the watery graveyard of unearthed bodies, and enough explosives to level Tokyo—no. Didn't see anything out of the ordinary at all."

"Damn."

Interest piqued, Brinks asked, "Why?"

"No reason."

The kid's words suddenly came to mind: *There's something out there.*

"What the hell happened out there, Ron? What were they doing in that underwater station?" Between the surfaced shrapnel and the kid claiming to see a giant shark and the two events taking place within close proximity of each other, Brinks assumed the two incidents were related. Brinks knew Petruski's company funded unsanctioned scientific experiments that often included illegal dealings of varying sorts, otherwise they wouldn't have built a submarine station in the middle of nowhere, outside of US-owned waters. Whatever they were doing down there, whatever they were into, had backfired.

Escaped.

As a man who chose his words carefully, Ronald took his time answering. "Don't know the details. All I know, whatever it was, it went wrong."

"No shit." He glanced over his shoulder, making sure eavesdroppers weren't looming near. "Look, we found this kid. Floating in the water. He was out there about a day. Claims he saw a shark."

"Well, there are sharks out there." A bitter laugh. "Wouldn't surprise me."

Brinks wiped away a layer of sweat from his brow. "No. Not any shark. A big one. Man-eater. Fucking giant. Claims his friend was consumed whole."

A troubled "hmm." Brinks thought the untrustworthy bastard would laugh him off again, but he ended up surprising him. "Guess it's true then."

"What's true?"

"About Petruski and what he was up to in the deep."

Brinks's fingers tightened around the telephone. "And what was he up to, Ronald?" he asked through gritted teeth.

"Fucked if I know. Rumor has it, he discovered a new species at the bottom of the Gulf while one of his oil companies was drilling. Something no one ever heard about, something they could not find in any biology textbook. No one knows much else than that. Some local marine biologists and universities wanted in on the discovery, but Petruski shut them all out. Wanted the fame all for himself. Although it's been years and he's never officially come forth with what it was they found down there." A brief pause while Ronald sucked down a cancerous fog. "I thought it was bullshit. But if what that kid said is true, I don't know— maybe he discovered some dinosaur-shark or something."

"That's very informative. Sounds like a bad sci-fi movie."

"Well, sometimes the truth is stranger than fiction."

"Whatever the fuck it is doesn't change our quandary— stranded on this fucking island in the middle of fucking nowhere."

"Nowhere is better than somewhere," Ron said. "Especially if Petruski is after you. Believe me."

And he did believe him. Only Brinks was not one to run, especially with his pride and reputation hanging in the balance. "Whoever rigged those explosives is still out there. Probably hunting down the shark. Petruski isn't going to leave a thread hanging, you said so yourself. Am I right to assume that?"

"That'd be a safe bet." Brinks pictured the greasy chimp on the other end of the phone shrugging. "Although, it'd be safer to assume the mess has been purified. Petruski doesn't fuck around when it comes to calamities such as this. Something you should have learned by now."

"Thanks for the info, Ronald. I'll be sure to pay you a visit once I get off this turd of an island."

The brittle laugh that followed penetrated his ear so deeply, the vibration coated his brain. "Good luck, dead man," Ronald said, and then he was gone.

12.

Evan stared at his laptop with sheer astonishment. Opening his mouth, his brain simply couldn't come up with the words. Monica and Ally hung over his shoulder, hands on their knees, squinting, trying to catch a glimpse of what Evan claimed he had seen.

"What is it?" Monica asked.

Evan swallowed. He'd begun to sweat and not because of the bright, blinding sun. "Sh-shark."

"A bull shark?" Ally asked, chipper as ever. She bounced on her heels.

Evan shook his head.

Monica tapped him on the shoulder. "A hammerhead," she said with confidence, turning back to Ally. "Remember how we saw a couple last year. They must be—"

"Wasn't a hammerhead," Evan said, adjusting the screen to fight off the glare.

"What the hell was it then?"

Brow ruffled, Evan slowly made his way to his feet. He turned to the girls, his face white as printer paper. The girls stepped away, the two of them wondering if their classmate was going to lose his fish taco lunch. "I think we need to get the professor."

"Um, you don't look so good, dude," Monica told him.

"I saw…"

What had I seen?

He'd seen teeth. A huge mouth. *That body. The enormity of it.* If it was a shark—and he was confident it was—it was the biggest shark he'd ever seen. The biggest shark on the goddamn planet.

That color. That black skin.

He was sure he'd seen a black shark, which wasn't possible because there were no black sharks, not out here.

Maybe it wasn't a shark. May it was a… a…

A whale? Evan supposed it could have been a whale, but he got a very good look at the sea monster's jaws, and they definitely resembled that of a shark, a Great White to be specific.

The girls stared at him, their eyebrows arched.

"I don't know," he finally said. "I think it was a shark."

"You think?" Monica asked, the corners of her mouth curling. "How did Professor Pickard choose you for this, again?" She rolled her eyes. "Please tell me the school isn't giving you an academic scholarship. I mean, once they find out you can't tell what a shark looks like…"

Ally clicked her tongue. "Knock it off, Monica."

She stuck her tongue out at her friend. Ally giggled.

"No," Evan said, pointing to the screen. "It *was* a shark. Big. And black."

Wrinkles fixed Monica's forehead. "Black? You're saying you saw a black shark?" Forced laughter erupted from her throat. Stifling the outburst, she added, "Yeah, and I'm the newest Kardashian."

Evan turned, the color in his face ruddying. "I'm not dicking around!"

They faced the laptop in time to see a shadow materialize in the distance. Evan whipped around and planted himself in the hot sand. He took the controller and guided the fake seal toward the dark presence. The girls leaned over his shoulders, shooting each other dubious looks. They didn't truly believe their classmate, but Evan had always been academically minded, never much of a prankster. Jokes and other foolery weren't his thing, despite what the dreadlocks and marijuana-scented cologne might suggest. If the kid had seen a black shark, then he had seen a black shark. Or at the very least, *believed* he had.

The shadow quickly took on a form. Dark. Bulky. Lengthy. Its mass was too big for the GoPro to capture. At first, the girls thought they were looking at the silhouette of a Great White, its features all too similar. But as their rubber seal engaged, nearing the creature of titanic length, they realized they were looking at a much bigger monster, and one that wasn't white.

"Holy shit," Monica said, her words followed with a sharp gasp.

Evan tapped the screen. In a nervous whisper, he said, "Told you."

The shark darted out of view before the three could further examine it. The movement caused them to jump, as if they expected the shark to leap off the screen at them. In reality, the maneuver didn't make sense, didn't register with their brains. How could a shark of that size move with such agility? It didn't add up. Great Whites could boogie, sure, but not like that. It had moved like a tadpole.

Evan felt ill. As his view of the world took on a slight twirl, he rotated the seal around one-hundred-and-eighty degrees.

"Where the hell did it go?" Monica asked.

Evan ignored her along with the rest of the world. Nothing else existed except what was on the screen and the strange notions overtaking his thoughts. He knew getting the professor was probably protocol, although he doubted there was such a rule written for these circumstances. His instincts told him to run and find Pickard, but something else held him in front of that computer screen.

I've done it, he thought. *I've discovered a new species!*

He continued spinning the seal around, the camera picking up on nothing but clear waters and beams of sunlight cutting through the surface. Once he made several turns, he thought about driving the seal back to shore, thinking the shark had disappeared with no intention of reappearing. Besides, he seriously needed to get Pickard, show the professor the tape and let him make any and all decisions. He wondered what Pickard would say when he showed him the evidence.

The second he pulled down on the controller's directional thumbstick, two rows of sharp teeth filled the screen. The image lasted no longer than a second before cutting to black, but it would remain burned in three students' brains for as long as they lived.

"Holy shit!" Monica screamed.

Evan, who had retreated from the laptop like a crab, now laid himself down on the sand and stared at the endless blue above. He couldn't decide which was worse: losing the seal, or the fact that there was a massive, bloodthirsty killing machine no more than two miles offshore.

Ally shivered. "Did I just see what I think I saw?"

"We need to get the professor down here," Evan said. "Now."

"On it," replied Ally. Despite what she'd just seen, she still managed to sound lively. She rushed back toward the villa, sprinting as if she were on the last leg of a metered dash.

"You know," Monica said, crouching beside Evan. "This is kind of thrilling."

Evan peeled his hands away from his face. Monica's smile looked down at him.

"This is some serious stuff," he told her. "I don't want to speculate, dude, but I think we just found a new species. Something…" The word prehistoric came to mind, but he knew how ridiculous that would sound out loud. "Something big."

"Let's keep ourselves grounded. We still haven't seen this thing in person yet."

Evan swallowed. "Are you sure you want to?"

Still smiling, she nodded.

Evan wondered if she'd still think so later with her body compressed between the beast's massive jaws, mangled beyond recognition.

13.

Brinks returned with three cold bottles of water. He tossed one to Gardner who snatched it out of the air with an effortless swipe. Then he cracked one open for the kid. CJ tore the bottle away from him like a hungry infant, half of its contents gone in less than ten seconds.

"Easy, kid," Brinks warned, pulling the bottle back. "Little at a time."

"Thirsty."

"Yeah, I get it. Bet you never heard of hyponatrenia."

CJ shook his head.

"Too much too fast could cause salt levels in your blood to drop. Potentially dangerous. Seen a man hospitalized for a week from it. Not pretty."

Gardner chuckled. "That's why he's the boss, kid. Motherfucker knows everything."

Brinks smirked, continuing to address CJ. "Plus, we need to make our supplies last. I don't know how long we're going to be stuck here."

CJ nodded. He rested his back on the concrete and closed his eyes. He fell asleep the second his head hit the ground.

Gardner pointed his chin at Rudders'. "Any luck?"

"Well, bad news is that we can't afford a room. Good news is that I made a phone call." Brinks sipped from his bottle. "You were right. Fucking island rednecks."

"Fucking-A." Gardner squinted against the sun. "So what did that rat-faced fuck Ronny have to say for himself?"

"Nothing that would please you very much."

"Takes a lot to please me these days." He chewed his tongue. "Lemme guess: the douche didn't know we were about to get burned?"

"Something like that. I get the strong suspicion he was in on it. Don't worry, I promised him we'd pay his ass a visit when we got back to the mainland." He surveyed his surroundings. *If we get back to the mainland.*

"Did he sound scared?"

"Not one bit, which bothers me to some degree. Thought I had a good reputation."

"You've gotten soft over the years."

"Have I?"

"Hanson always thought so." Gardner's eyes took on a sparkly sheen. "Damn. I almost forgot we just lost him."

Brinks sighed. "Gardner, I'm so goddamn sorry. I knew how close you two were."

He shook his head. "Don't sweat it. I know how it is. Every mission could be our last. Fuck, I mean, we've been through so much shit, it's kind of a miracle we made it this long."

"Still, doesn't make it any easier."

"Nope." Gardner eyed the sea, the waves becoming more aggressive as they spoke. "Sure doesn't."

"Our revenge will be sweet. I promise." Brinks used his hand as a visor and followed Gardner's gaze. "But we need to find a way off Gilligan's Island before we do any-goddamn-thing."

"Any luck with that?"

"Well, we could go back in and ask for a ride."

Gardner shook his head. "Uh-uh. I don't fuck with island rednecks. Told you."

"So where does that leave us?"

Gardner's eyes found the edge of the cliff. He'd seen what was below it, same as Brinks. "I say we get creative."

"Commandeer a ship?"

"Dunno what the fuck that means, but if it's along the lines of Grand Theft Aqua, then I'm game."

Brinks patted his friend on the shoulder. "Most of the men inside are either drunk or well on their way. Doubt any of them will be navigating the seas anytime soon. Should give us plenty of time to skedaddle."

"Sounds good to me."

"You can drive a boat, can't you?"

"Shit, my daddy used to take us fishing every weekend." A wide smile returned to his face. "Course I can."

Brinks, whose daddy only took him to strip clubs and scuzzy Atlantic City casinos every other weekend, didn't know the difference between a gunwale or a starboard. "Okay then. Let's get a move on."

"One question though."

"What's that?"

Gardner looked down at CJ, who had fallen asleep during their conversation. "Who carries the kid?"

Brinks sighed, long and hard. "I got an idea." He walked over to the kid and knelt down. Grabbing the kid's arms, he said, "We did our good deed for the day. Right? I mean, God won't hold it against us, will He?"

"He better not," Gardner said, gripping the kid's ankles. "Or me and Him, we'll have words."

14.

"This is crazy," Evan said, two feet on the dock, the other two gripping the charter boat railing. "You can't just go looking for this thing!"

Professor Pickard jumped down from the second deck shelter, landing limber on the main deck. "Ally, can you go grab the laptop?" he asked. "I think we left it on the beach."

Ally nodded, then jumped onto the dock. She sprinted off towards the laptop.

"I have to agree with Evan here," Jill said, pacing the edge of the wharf, hands tucked under her arms.

Pickard shot her an icy glare. *Get lost,* his eyes practically screamed. "Well, no one asked you, Jill."

"Okay then." She threw her arms in the air. "Are you trying to impress me? Is that it? You think going after this shark is going to win me over? Make me feel all warm and cuddly inside? Bring back the reasons of why I lov—" She stopped herself. Every eye turned on her and she grew increasingly nervous. She almost didn't continue. Her throat seized as the words came, however, she pushed through it. "Of why I... why I *liked* you."

"I don't care how it makes you feel."

Evan made that awkward daddy-and-mommy-are-fighting face. He slowly backed away, halfway down the dock. None of his warnings to Pickard had made much of a difference anyway. His professor was acting like a stubborn fool.

"Don't be stupid, Neil."

"Who are you to tell me how to act?"

Taken aback, Jill smirked. "You're really doing this?"

Monica poked her head from below deck. "Sonar is ready to go, professor."

He turned with a smile. "Thank you, Monica."

Two seconds later, Ally returned with the laptop. She handed the machine to Pickard who accepted it with anxious hands.

He winked at her.

Jill's blood bubbled. Her fists closed. She clenched them until her knuckles went white. She closed her eyes and tried to think of happy thoughts, but the sunshine and hovering angels her mind conjured quickly turned into turbulent tornadoes and dancing devils. She couldn't help it; she hated the bastard. He brought out the worst in her.

And yet, you came here willingly, her inner self-informed her. She was still trying to figure that one out herself. Not one of her best decisions, though her dead mother would argue poor choices were the norm.

There's just something about him. Something about the way he makes me feel.

Right now he was making her feel like absolute shit.

She snarled. "If you're expecting me to pull some if-you're-going-I'm-going bullshit, it ain't happening, Pickard."

He spread his arms wide, inviting her best shot. "Go ahead. Stay. Go. Don't matter to me."

"You call in my ride?" she asked, knowing he probably hadn't. "Someone coming to get me?"

His arms fell at his sides. A great gust of air whooshed past his lips. "You're going to have to wait till tomorrow morning. Sunup."

She stomped her foot on the pier. "Goddammit, Neil!"

"It's the best I could do!" he shouted back.

"Children!" Monica said from below. She poked her head up, reminding Jill of that silly gopher from *Caddyshack.* The girl faced her teacher and flashed him a great big smile. "We're ready to go, professor. Whaddya say? Shark hunt?"

Pickard looked from Monica to Jill. "Last chance, Jill. You coming?"

"Fuck no," she said, then stormed back down the boardwalk, toward the beach and away from her problems.

* * *

Once Jill was gone, Monica said, "Your old girlfriend's a real bitch."

Pickard ignored her. "Come on, he said. Let's get going." Before they pulled away from the dock, he turned to Ally and Evan and said, "Keep her company. Don't let her do anything... *drastic.*"

They shrugged as though they had been asked a question to which they had no answer.

Pickard took that as a "sure thing" and thanked them, put the charter in gear, motored away from the shore, and propelled them to where Evan thought he saw the shark attack their faux seal.

15.

At first, the kid looked dead. Eddie Rudders sucked on his cigarette, contemplating what to do with the body if his suspicions were true. The unconscious kid's skin glistened with sweat and oozing open sores. Eddie kicked the kid in the sun-scabbed shoulder with his toe, a gentle attempt to wake him up. His flesh was soft, almost as if it would cave in if he pressed harder. The kid didn't move, not so much as a twitch.

Great, how the hell am I going to explain this to the authorities? Eddie thought, taking another drag, long and pleasing.

There had never been a dead body on Key Water Island before without the last name Rudders. Least not to Eddie's knowledge, although much of what he remembered from family history had been wiped clean by drug and alcohol abuse. Eddie had spent a great deal of his twenties and thirties on the mainland, experimenting with things like meth, heroin, and crack cocaine. He drank heavily. Got laid a lot. Lots of women. Men, too. Ah, the mainland years.

Since he turned forty, Eddie turned his life around. He came back home and surprisingly enough, his parents accepted him back. Even gave him a job tending the bar. That was his only job, besides the odds and ends things such as general maintenance and handymen chores.

Abstaining from alcohol had been his biggest challenge. The crank habit he was able to kick easily. He'd never considered himself an "addict" and found leaving the drugs behind an effortless struggle. That wasn't the case with booze. He figured not seeing a wax foil of dope in almost ten years had something to do with it. On the other hand, he was face-to-face with old buddy Jack Daniels every single night. He often thought about breaking the vow to himself and getting shitfaced along with his patrons. But something held him back. Something inside him repelled the dark knot in the center of his chest, that empty hole that begged to be fed.

But now, as he peered down at the dead-ish kid, he wanted not only to drink from every bottle behind the bar, but shoot his veins full of sweet narcotics as well.

He quickly pushed away images of a needle disappearing under his tender flesh and mused about what to do about the kid. He'd seen dead bodies in the sleazy back alleys of Miami, but not on Key Water Island. Fish, sure. They washed up all the time. Heck, just last winter Eddie and his brothers found a hammerhead that had washed up on the eastern side of the hotel. Derek, Eddie's younger, smarter brother, explained to him the effects of global warming on the climate, and how that initiated cataclysmic changes in the ocean's ecosystem. Eddie zoned out after a few minutes of his intelligent babble, so he didn't remember quite how the story went. Regardless, that had nothing to do with the kid whose body was marred with sun blisters.

Eddie thought maybe the kid had something to do with the university's side of the island. Maybe the kid was partying too hard last night, got lost in the jungle, found his way to the other side of the island, and fell asleep on the Rudders' property.

Died, Eddie corrected himself. *Died.*

No, that wasn't right. If he looked closely enough, he'd see the kid's chest rise and fall. He wasn't dead. Comatose, but not dead.

Then he noticed he wasn't from the university. At the kid's side, rested a half-empty bottle of water, one of three that Eddie had given the strange new patron not more than twenty minutes ago. The mysterious man who had entered the bar, asking to phone the mainland free of charge. *The stranger.* Rudders saw few strangers over the years. This man had taken him by surprise, especially considering the rips and holes throughout his all-black clothing, which looked oddly military. Yeah, the man had put the *strange* in stranger, all right. Eddie wondered what the man and this unconscious kid were doing here, and why the kid had been left behind. He figured it was something he didn't need to involve himself in.

And he'd be right.

Eddie sat down, propping his back against the T1-11 siding. As he enjoyed the last few puffs of his smoke, he glanced over at the pallet of paint buckets. He wasn't looking forward to his weekend chore—painting the entire exterior of the hotel. Mother and Father always handed him the shitty work, and even though he complained, it never got him anything except shittier jobs.

A coastal breeze brushed his long black hair across his face. He sucked in another ashy lungful, and watched the wind carry off a small cloud away from his nose.

The kid's back jumped off the ground and he sat upright, sucking in gasps of air.

"Great buckets of shark shit!" Eddie cried out, the shrunken remains of his cigarette falling from his fingers.

The kid turned to him, huffing in short breaths. "Where am I?" He coughed. Eyes darting nervously, he spotted the half-empty bottle of water beside him, snatched it up, unscrewed the cap, and started chugging.

"Yer at Rudders'."

The kid swigged the last mouthful, then raised the bottle away from his lips, allowing the last few drops to rain down on his forehead. "Rudders'?"

"Yes."

CJ looked around. "Did you see two men?"

Eddie's eyes shifted side to side. "Two men?"

"Men. In all black."

Eddie nodded. "Didn't see two. Only one. Came into the bar about twenty minutes ago. Made a phone call. His face was cut up. Bleeding. Didn't think to ask him any questions. The way I saw it, it was none of my business." Eddie swallowed a hard, invisible lump. He didn't know how to proceed and had grown increasingly nervous. He sensed danger afoot. "Name's Eddie. Eddie Rudder. My parents own the bar, and mostly everything else on Key Water Island. They aren't here right now. Took my brothers for a weekend getaway to New Orleans."

The kid seemed disinterested. Eddie's heart hammered against the walls of his chest. The phantom taste of alcohol graced his lips. He felt an imaginary burn ski down his throat.

CJ grimaced and pushed himself to his knees. Eddie watched him search for the strength to lift himself to his feet, the kid struggling to summon the last shred of power wasted on his previous effort. Instead, he fell back on his hands and crab-walked until he was against the hotel's exterior. Once his back met the siding, he used what was left in his tank to stand himself up. His knees quivered like thin tree branches getting whipped in a tropical storm. The kid winced, his muscles clearly protesting their usage. The maneuver seemed to have zapped him of all his energy. Using the hotel's exterior for support, CJ steadied his breathing and looked down at Eddie.

"You okay, kid?" Eddie asked, looking up at him. He surveyed every cut and boil on the kid's exposed flesh. "Anything I can get for you?"

Closing his eyes, nodded slowly. "Yes. You can get me off this island, and as far away from here as possible."

16.

Her dorsal fin surfaced, cutting through the blue with swift, calculated speed. The hunt was on.

She had circled the island several times. There had been good meals, and meals that weren't so appetizing. The fake seal had been an infuriating experience. It tasted awful and luckily she had been keen enough not to have swallowed it. She didn't think it would have wreaked havoc on her internal organs, but she did worry about her young. After all, she was eating for four now. What she ate, they ate, too.

The fake seal stewed in her thoughts. She knew it was manmade. Humans playing their tricks, their games, trying to reel her in, bring her back to a life of pain and suffering and slavery. She was far too intelligent to fall for their ruse.

Instead of lingering, she swam to the other side of the island. There, she tangled with a school of blue fish, which she hunted and eviscerated with ease. Their meat barely did anything to satiate her. She felt her swollen belly dance with delight as the fish meat went down, sending nutrition to her young. They drained the nutrients and when they were finished, there was hardly any sustenance left for mama. God, they were hungry critters. Hungry and growing at an alarming rate. She could almost feel them lengthening by the minute. No, by the second. So quickly, she started to wonder if her belly might burst within the hour.

They were almost ready.

Their birth would come soon.

And then the lands of this planet would belong to them.

She pressed on, trapping a sizable tuna with the right corner of her maw, clamping down, reveling in the blood that swirled before her like exploding cosmic dust. Once devoured, she moved onto the next meal. A hammerhead. It smelled her coming from a mile away, but it didn't start to panic until its eyes beheld her titanic anatomy. The hammerhead tried to escape, thrashing through the waters, diving into the deep where it figured the Ocean Queen couldn't go because of its considerable bulk. As it descended, the hammerhead started thrashing around wildly, darting whichever way its squirrelly mind instructed, as if some interior force muddled its thoughts. The deep of the darkest variety seemed to have an adverse effect on the hammerhead's motor functions. The Ocean Queen speculated this with delight, drawing the conclusion that these depths were not meant for it.

The hunt was hardly fair after that. The Ocean Queen sailed over the frantic shark like a black cloud of apocalyptic proportions. Less than ten seconds later, the hammerhead found itself in the clutches of her powerful jaws, wriggling and whipping its body, futile zero-hour desperation. With one powerful crunch, the hammerhead's insides squirted through the ragged opening on its midsection. Mashed viscera and clouds of blood twirled in the bubbly rush of agitated water, and the Ocean Queen knew that was the last image the hammerhead took in before losing itself to the darkness of her gullet.

That happy notion didn't satisfy the grumble in her belly.

Still hungry, the Ocean Queen searched on.

She surfaced again on the eastern side of the island. She sensed more movement in the water. A cold breeze blew over her, sending a chill across her dorsal fin, down her interdorsal ridge. As she neared the shore, she saw what populated the water, what attracted her toward the coast. Boats. Manmade methods of transportation. She slipped beneath the surface, hoping none of those pesky lifeforms spotted her. Whatever she was planning, the element of surprise would be crucial.

Her thoughts wandered away from the humans and their sick torture devices back to her home-world, or what had been her home world, the derelict remains of that crippled planet. Would she ever return? No, probably not. The land had dried up, their main resources evaporated. Her kind needed water, depended on it for survival. On this planet water was plentiful. The blue world she explored was enough to support millions of her kind.

She wondered about her babies. Would they be shark? Would they be Ha'La'Ra? Would they be something else? She speculated whether the humans' tests would affect their birth. They had poked and prodded her, injected her with foreign fluids, syringes full of materials alien to her and her system. She supposed the injections could alter her DNA and possibly damage her young, render them intellectually feeble. Or worse—provoke a miscarriage. She hoped not. The notion instigated a rage inside her, bringing forth the fury of a thousand storms.

She promised herself: once this was over and the babies were born, she'd kill the humans. All of them. Every last one. They didn't deserve this utopia. They were leeches, sucking the planet dry of its vitals. They didn't know how to respect it. How to treat it. The Ocean Queen had learned from her planet's mistakes. The upper echelon responsible for leading her home-world had been much of the same, taking the planet and its resources for granted. Leaving nothing left for the future. Things would be different here. She'd make sure of it. She'd teach her young to respect the planet. Treat her nicely. Embrace nature, not destroy it. Not exhaust every resource. Not bleed the earth dry, blanketing it with desolation.

But first, she'd render the humans extinct, obliterate the biggest plight on the planet. It would be her gift to the new world.

And her young would see it through.

She could hear them agreeing with her, chirping with savage delight.

Suddenly her head was filled with voices. Above the surface. She glided her massive frame toward the sound. Staying just below the surface, she headed for the shore where the boats rested, knocking around in the choppy waters. The sun threw down tunnels of light, which disappeared under her. The warmth of the water felt good. A pleasurable sensation skated down her back. She couldn't tell if the anticipation of violence was partially responsible for her lively mood, but suspected it might be.

The Ocean Queen spotted two men above the surface. She heard the warbling of their conversation. She didn't speak the human language, didn't understand a word of it. But she knew what boats were, what purpose they served. They moved across the surface of the water. They went places. Faraway places. Lands abound.

She decided these humans would never arrive at their destination. None of the humans on Key Water Island would. She would keep them there, for when the time came to give birth and come ashore, there would be plenty of food.

The ultimate feast awaited.

17.

"Stupid turds left the keys in the ignition," Gardner said, standing before the control panel on a medium-sized fishing charter. He went to twist the key when Brinks gripped his shoulder. He stopped and turned to his boss. "What is it?"

"You crank that engine and you'll alert our friends in the bar." Brinks pointed his chin up to the top of the crag. Above, gulls circled like sharks in the sky. "A clean getaway is preferable. Don't want them running after us with pitchforks."

"Bro. We got guns."

"Guns that spent a lot of time underwater. Who knows if they'll even fire."

Gardner made a face suggesting someone stuffed his mouth with lemons. "You know they will."

Brinks shook his head. "Point is, we don't want to draw any attention to ourselves."

His subordinate shrugged. He saluted Brinks. "Whatever you say, boss man."

Brinks made his way around the stern, located the rope, and began tugging the anchor aboard.

Gardner set his weapon down on the starboard and glanced over the dials in front of him. A thousand memories came flooding back to him, all those weekends spent on the bay, fishing with his father and siblings. Best times of his life, sans the Goon Squad years. Completely different spectrum of feelings, but he cherished those dangerous missions on the other side of the world all the same. Even the ones that had gone completely FUBAR. The ones that left him with scars, emotionally and physically.

Damn, he thought, *those were some good times.*

Those thoughts quickly transformed into memories of Hanson, his brother-from-another-mother. He wished Hanson was by his side now. He cursed himself. It was all his fault. He'd been greedy. Too greedy. But smart. If it weren't Hanson, then it would have been his ass blown to pieces.

But he'd made a deal with the devil. Now he had to live with the consequences.

Dammit, man. He remembered Hanson when he first met the fucker. He was from the backwoods of Alabama. Gardner from the New York suburbs. Two different walks of life. Somehow, they connected. Became best friends. And much more.

Lovers.

Gardner was pretty sure Brinks knew, although the two men had been overly discrete about their arrangements. He knew Brinks had a strange sixth sense about things, had a nose for sniffing out secret information. Gardner didn't care much. He knew the relationship wouldn't last given their occupation. Loyalty seldom lasted in this line of work. It was all about the green paper and how many zeroes you could cash. He'd been around the game long enough to see the score. Sooner or later, the Good Squad would disband.

Gardner just wanted to make sure his future was financially secure when they did.

And what was wrong with that?

Traitor.

"Gardy?" Brinks said from the opposite end of the boat. "You okay?"

Gardner unburdened his thoughts. He felt himself sweating. "Yeah, boss."

"Anchor's up. Get ready to—"

Gardner reached behind his back and removed the two-shooter tucked against the base of his spine.

Brinks read the situation before Gardner steadied his aim. He was already moving to the edge of the boat.

That damn sixth sense, Gardner thought, curling his finger around the trigger and squeezing.

(POP POP)

The shots sounded off but not before Brinks hurled himself over the side of the boat. One of the bullets caught him somewhere in the upper chest area; a wet crimson cloud misted into the atmosphere above his airborne body. An instant later, he heard Brinks's body slap against the water. Instead of turning for the controls and getting a head start before the angry mob appeared at the edge of the cliff, he sprinted to the spot where Brinks went over. He looked down at the water and saw turbulent crimson waves knocking against the boat. He watched the space for a full minute, waiting for the water to calm, for Brinks to resurface. But he never did. Knowing Brinks couldn't hold his breath for longer than ninety seconds, Gardner inhaled a sigh of relief and turned away from the bloody fog that claimed the clarity of the tropical ocean below.

As he jogged back to the controls, he wondered where exactly the bullet had entered Brinks. His chest? Lungs? Did he pierce the motherfucker's heart? God, he hoped so. He also hoped Petruski didn't require proof of death other than his good word.

The second Gardner reached the control panel, the moment before he gripped the key with the intention of cranking the motor, something monstrous emerged from the water. He turned in time to witness an enormous black shape crashing down on the dock, snapping the wooden walkway in half, reducing the long boards to splinters. The sounds of destruction reminded him of a sharp crack of thunder on a humid summer night. Like the sky had ripped in half. The savage impact tossed debris into the air. Deck splinters rained down on him, along with the misty droplets from the small wave that violently rocked his ride back and forth to the point where Gardner thought he might capsize. The aggressive motion wasn't enough to overturn the boat, but it did sweep his feet out from under him, causing his head to crack open upon its collision with the starboard. Numbness crawled over his skull. He opened his eyes and saw incarnadine seep into his vision. His face was wet with red. He pressed his palm against the sharp, searing pain on his forehead. He found himself wearing a scarlet glove of blood.

Panic set in.

He knew what the black shape had been. *The shark. Holy shit, the kid wasn't lying!*

Not only was he bleeding profusely from a potentially life-threatening injury, but now there was an apex predator stalking the surrounding waters. Gardner knew he was in trouble. The bad kind. Not the kind he was used to.

Because you're alone. You killed your friends, the only ones who could save you.

He ignored his conscience and scrambled to his feet,

immediately searching the deck for the first aid box. He thought about firing up the motor and getting the hell out of there before the shark smelled Brinks's blood in the water, but he wouldn't get very far if he passed out from shock or blood loss. He figured if he could slow the bleeding, it would at least give him enough time to get back to the mainland and seek proper medical attention.

He surveyed the deck. No first aid box. He rose to his feet without the help of his hands, both of which were applied to the leaky gash over his right eye. His attention was stolen by the sight of the dock, or what was left of it. Wasn't much. The shark had destroyed most of it with one belly flop. Knowing the beast was swimming nearby, plotting its next move, Gardner turned back to the controls, abandoning his search for the medical supplies. He'd have to do without.

Rushing toward the key, he heard splashing from somewhere close. He hoped it was Brinks struggling with his dying breath, hoping the shark would see his old boss and concentrate its efforts there. Gardner tuned out the disturbed water and fixed his gaze on the key. Even though the wet deck threatened to take him down again, he reached the control panel safely.

He cranked the motor to life.

Somewhere above, he heard men shouting. He glanced over his shoulder. A small flock had gathered at the edge of the cliff. The fishermen were pointing down at him, screaming, cursing, demanding that he stop whatever the hell he was doing.

Gardner smiled back at them. He flipped them a bloody bird and shouted, "Fuck you, you island redneck motherfuckers!" Then he pushed the throttle forward. The boat sped off. Their cries and pleas drowned beneath the growl of the motor.

He got no more than fifty yards. The black shark appeared before him, its massive open jaws rising from the surface like some alien spacecraft ready to ascend the sky. But the monster didn't fly. It waited patiently for its meal.

Gardner cut the wheel and screamed until his throat ripped itself raw, both of which did him nothing. The front of the boat fit perfectly in the shark's gargantuan mouth. It closed its maw with the force of an industrial compactor, reducing the cruiser to half its size. Fragments of wood and fiberglass and specks of watered-down blood flew, shooting into the air like a frenzy of death flies. The rest of the boat shuddered and Gardner lost his balance for a second time, found himself tumbling across the deck.

During the chaos, the black shark disappeared under the tumultuous waves.

Gardner had no time to thank God for sparing him; the shark exploded from the water, its massive frame gliding through the air beautifully, just like Gardner had seen on those cool nature documentaries.

Fucking Shark Week.

He didn't like the show now that he was living in one.

The black shark landed on the rear of the boat, tipping it like a seesaw. Gardner felt himself go, slide back. He desperately grabbed for something—*anything*—that would keep him from chuting into the shark's death trap. He managed to hook his arm around a nearby handle, the boat's equivalent to his sedan's oh-shit bar. With every shred of strength he could summon, he held on.

The shark chewed on the air between Gardner's feet and its maw, opening and closing its jowls like a baby bird accepting its first worm from mama.

Gardner felt his strength slip. "No, no, no, no," he repeated, as if it were some personal mantra.

The shark's bloody snout pushed forward. Snapping its jaws, it wormed its way up the deck, toward Gardner's kicking feet. Tears streamed from the corners of his eyes. He knew it was only a matter of time before his strength failed him. Only a matter of time before the shark won.

He'd never seen a shark of this size before. Its labial furrows stretched, its mouth a doorway into an opaque world. The shark's skin was dark as midnight, galaxy black to match its soulless eyes. This was no shark. It was some prehistoric monster. Something archaic. Something from a time long since passed. This animal didn't belong here. Not in this era. Not in these waters. As Gardner felt his fingers slip, his last bit of power abandoning his body, he wondered what epoch gave birth to this beast.

Or what planet.

As he slid toward its open jaws, he tried to put both feet on the shark's bullet-shaped snout, hoping to use it as a springboard. It was a desperate attempt and Gardner knew he was only prolonging the inevitable. He managed to get one foot high enough. The other foot landed in the bloody abyss filled with row after row of sharp, saw-like teeth. The shark chomped down, squeezing Gardner's leg between its powerful aperture. Gardner howled. He clawed at the shark's skin, dragging his fingernails across its black rubbery coating. Once he realized how benign that was, he stretched for the eyeball on the right side of its head. The shark repositioned its grip on Gardener's leg, biting closer to the groin. Hot blood spurted from the area like water from the end of a fire hose. A new world of pain introduced itself to Gardener. The atmosphere darkened, nearly flickered out. He held onto the light, what little remained, and reached, his fingers dancing along the beast's slick skin, attempting to locate its ocular cavity. Gardner touched it, that slimy oval, and dug his fingers in.

The shark thrashed its head back and forth, whipping Gardener with fury. The shark made no noise, but Gardner knew it felt pain. Determined, he sunk his fingers deeper until they were completely inside the monstrous fish's head. Scooping out the eyeball like a cherry from a small jar, Gardener's small victory brought forth laughter. It sounded far away, like the echoes of old dreams.

The shark, no longer amused by the hunt, opened its jaws, letting gravity work its magic, letting the human sink deeper into its mouth. Once half of his body slipped inside, the shark closed its clam with force, cracking bones and riddling his flesh with punctures and tears. Blood poured out of every new orifice and there was so much of it in the water, the men watching from above barely saw any blue in their peripherals.

Gardner let the pain in, stepping outside his thoughts and allowing the agony to eat away at him. As the shark dragged him below the surface, he relaxed his muscles and abandoned all hope. He wished the pain over and begged for death to come whisk him away.

Soon, an all-encompassing black curtain draped over him.

* * *

She left small portions of human meat behind in clouds of rust. It had tasted pretty good, and the imprisoned lifeforms within agreed. They were almost at the end, almost ready for freedom. Before nightfall, they'd be their own force, their own shapes and sizes. Free to roam their new world, their future dominion. She wondered how long it would take for them to conquer. Domination was a numbers game, she knew, so they'd have to reproduce quickly. But they also required food. That was paramount. They'd need their strength. The world was vast and seemingly endless. This island was just a small sample of how big the world really was.

And waiting on that island was a bountiful feast.

She decided to flee the violent scene, leave the remaining bits of human for the bottom feeders and head back to the other side of the island. There were fewer humans there, maybe none. The perfect place for an uninterrupted delivery.

The perfect place to usher in the new age.

The Time of the Ha'La'Ra.

18.

"Whatever it was," Monica said, staring at the radar, "it isn't here now."

Pickard looked out across the Gulf, using his left hand as an awning to block out sunlight. "Damn it."

Scraps of the GoPro and bits of the rubber seal had surfaced. The equipment was destroyed beyond repair. *Great,* Pickard scolded himself. *How am I going to explain that to the department?*

Monica frowned. When she spoke, her voice came out unbalanced. Shaky. "We should head back in, teach."

Pickard ignored her request and wandered over to the stern. Glimpsing back at the shore, he saw nothing but gentle waters, the occasional series of choppiness. From the surface, you'd never guess there was a seventy-foot shark patrolling below. His face burned from a strong gust of wind and something else. He felt a sudden rush of anger. Cheated, as if the world somehow wronged him. He hammered the ledge of the boat with his fists.

"Something wrong, teach?" Monica asked.

"Nothing, I just thought—"

"The shark—or whatever it is—isn't going anywhere. We can head back and tell the others what we found. Gather the necessary supplies. Get the authorities involved. You know, do it right."

Monica was the voice of reason, something Pickard usually ignored. He bit his lower lip. Maybe it was time to listen. He forced himself to grin. "I thought we could be the ones to discover it. On our own. No help from anyone else."

Monica checked her watch. "Well, we could phone FSU. Have them meet us here. They could bring supplies and… stuff."

Pickard shrugged like a child who had succumbed to not getting his way.

"Rome wasn't built in a day."

Pickard glared at her. "You're not helping, Monica."

Monica sauntered up behind him. She eyed the shore from over his shoulder. The villa was the size of a penny from this distance. "Think they can see us?"

She grabbed his waist, a hand on each hip. Her confidence had returned. She breathed hot air on his neck. Her hands migrated lower. And lower. And under his—

He spun around and shoved her away with more force than he had intended. Pursing his lips, he barked, "What the hell is wrong with you?"

Her face went slack with innocence. "What? Just trying to have a little fun, that's all."

He pointed a stern finger at her chest. "Well now isn't the time, nor is it the place."

For a few seconds she glared at him, then exploded with laughter. She threw her head back, cackling at the sky like some seventeenth-century sorceress. After she composed herself, she spoke sharply. "So now you want to act like a professor? Funny, you don't act so professional when you're fucking me from behind."

Pickard clenched his teeth so tightly he thought he might dislocate his jaw. "Monica. Listen to me. I'm not going to do this with you. Not here. Not now. Not with some aquatic behemoth swimming somewhere under us. Understand?"

She waved her hand in the air. "You're such an asshole. I better be getting a four-point-oh, or I'm going straight to the dean."

Pickard let go of his frustration with a drawn sigh. "You know I take care of you."

"Yeah. Me and all your girls." She shook her head. "What about her?" She nodded at the beach. Jill McCourty was just a speck. "You fucked her too, didn't you?"

Pickard didn't answer.

"Hm. I thought so. She hates you. You know that?"

He didn't want to indulge, but the answer fell from his mouth quicker than he could stop it. "Yes. I know."

"Sad. She actually seems nice under all that… bitchiness."

Pickard didn't respond. He looked back at the shore and thought of his wife, and how he had failed her. All the ways he failed as a husband, and there were many of them. For the first time in a long time, he actually felt disgusted with himself.

Monica held her hands out, impatiently waiting for instructions. "What are we doing, teach? Getting out of here?

Staying? Your call. I don't give a fuck anymore."

Pickard threw his head back to stretch the muscles in his neck. "Shit. What am I doing?"

"Huh?"

"What the fuck am I doing?"

"I don't know—"

"I love her."

Monica huffed, her eyes sweeping across the deck, unable to focus on him. "Who?"

"Jill. I love her."

"Oooh-kay. And why are you telling me?"

Pickard shook his head. He hadn't realized he'd spoken aloud. "I—what? I don't know. I—"

Monica flicked her wrist. "Okay, bozo. I'm done. Take me back. I'm getting out of here. You have more drama in your life than my grandmother's soap operas." She walked away from him, but not before shoving her middle finger in his face. "I can't believe I fu—"

Something splashed alongside the boat, killing the rest of Monica's speech.

They shared several moments of pure silence.

"What the fuck was that?" Monica said, gripping the first thing her hand could find: the chrome railing that bordered the cabin.

"I don't know." Pickard peeked over the railing. "Tuna maybe."

Before he had a chance to return his eyes to Monica with the intention of making everything better, a giant black hole lined with ivory daggers emerged from the water. Its enormous diameter swallowed up his vision.

In that moment he thought of Jill. Her face. Her body. There was a quick scene of their wedding day, an event that had only taken place in the private corners of his mind. He imagined kids playing at their feet while they kissed over meals they had cooked themselves. For the moment, time stood still and he experienced a life that never happened.

The life he truly wanted.

The weight of the beast's jaws snapped together, and before any amount of pain could register with his senses, an ethereal dark wave washed over his consciousness, sweeping him away forever.

* * *

Monica watched Pickard disappear inside the gargantuan black shark's mouth. It bit down, spraying gouts of blood across the deck. When the body of the beast collided with the boat, she was thrown forward, over the railing and into the blue.

Water rushed around her, a gush of bubbly foam. Her body froze in the wet, icy tomb. A numbing sensation cascaded down her spine, nestling against her bones. Unable to propel herself to the surface, she held her breath and waited for the inevitable. Saltwater found its way into her mouth and she swallowed every drop. She immediately opened her eyes, ignoring the slight burn, and searched for the colossal creature that had emerged from the darkest depths of the ocean and swallowed her hot professor whole.

Her vision was obscured by the swirling white rush of water and the drifting red wisps of Pickard's spilled blood. Panicked, she began to swim in the direction she thought the shore was located. She didn't get far. A seemingly infinite shadow sprawled over her, blocking out the sparkling rays of sunshine that had warmed her flesh. The sunlight had brought her tranquility, but that was soon replaced with the fear of being savagely torn apart. Darkness floated over her vision and the water became dim, dispiriting. She pretended like there wasn't a monster sailing over her and continued to paddle. A few strokes later, she closed her eyes, sensing the beast was toying with her, savoring its kill.

She wouldn't be some monster's plaything. She had already been Pickard's for far too long.

Sensing the end was near, she pushed herself, fast as she could, speeding toward the shore like the last lap of an Olympic swimming event. For a good ten seconds she paddled on, untouched. She started to feel good about her odds. Maybe the shark was full. No longer interested in her. Maybe those were storm clouds hanging over her head, not the lengthy mass of a kill-happy sea predator.

She opened her eyes in time to witness the opened crimson-stained maw of the shark, those jaws efficacious in annihilation, close down on her. Her frame was crushed under the powerful pressure, shattering her bones and shredding her flesh apart. The last thing she thought before her head burst like a water balloon, her brains escaping in tendrils of mush, was how she shouldn't have banged her teacher because if she hadn't then none of this would have happened.

* * *

The Ocean Queen settled near the bottom, just outside the shallows. Fish scattered as if their lives were in immediate danger, dipping and darting into the dimmest regions of the sea. The Ocean Queen had no use for fish. Not even larger ones, such as tunas or blue fish. Now she harbored the desire for human meat, a savory flavor no other could compare.

The time to give birth was coming. And fast. By nightfall, she'd deliver her young. Usher in a new hope for her species.

But first, she needed rest. She drifted out to sea, clinging to the deep, searching for a safe place to recoup. The killings had zapped too much energy from her, taken a toll on her pregnant body. A few hours of downtime and she'd find herself rejuvenated, ready to come ashore and do what she had been programmed to do.

Repopulate the Ha'La'Ra and take over the alien planet.

19.

From the balcony, Jill watched the entire event transpire. Her mouth was open, hoping—no, praying—her eyes had deceived her, that what she saw wasn't real. Her brain told her otherwise, informed her that what she witnessed was real, as true as anything she'd seen in all her life. Her legs weakened when she realized it wasn't her imagination. Pickard and Monica were gone, devoured by that beast—*that giant fucking shark*—black as an orca's skin.

Orca, she thought. Had it been a whale?

No, even from her distance and vantage point, she could make out the shark's features with clarity. There was no denying it. It was the biggest shark this planet had ever seen. Bigger than the Megalodon. More savage.

The teeth, she thought. *God, the teeth.* Rows of them. Perfect instruments of death.

Jill had been watching closely. Some might call it spying, but Jill called it watching. An argument had started between Pickard and his student, and that's when Jill's interest took hold. She had seen where Monica's hands migrated. She didn't need to read their lips. She saw what was happening. *She knew.* Knew because she had lived that life, experienced that situation for herself.

She sat down on a small trunk next to her bedroom door. She gathered her thoughts.

Well, you dumb bastard, you found your shark.

She tried to feel bad for Pickard. Tried to mourn his death. She couldn't. Thoughts in her head spiraled out of control. She thought about how she'd explain this to the authorities, explain this to *her* lieutenant.

She shook her head. Nothing came loose. She looked back at the destruction floating on the now gentle waters and wondered if she'd shed a tear for him when this was all over.

Get your shit together. You're a cop. Start acting like one.

She tried.

Standing up, she fought sunlight away from her face with the back of her hand. The two other students Pickard had put in harm's way sped down the dock. They were screaming, shouting, nothing articulate that Jill could make sense of. Evan kept looking over his shoulder, as if expecting to see the shark tailing him, obliterating the dock as he pursued his next meal. Ally didn't look back. She sprinted as if she *knew* the shark was right behind her.

They reached the villa's patio and bounded up the stairs, taking three and four at a time. They ran down the balcony toward Jill, who had done everything she could to wipe the anxiety clean from her expression.

"Did you see?" asked Ally, her chest heaving.

Slowly, Jill nodded.

"That thing," Evan said, his voice much higher than it had been before. "That thing… ate them."

Jill sighed. She was pacing back and forth, scratching her forehead. Breathing hard. It felt like her lungs were full of sand.

Breathless, Evan asked, "What do we do?"

"I don't know."

"What do you mean you don't know?"

Ally added, "Aren't you a cop?"

"Yes," Jill responded, "but…"

Her eyes widened.

"What is it?" Evan asked.

"Neil…" She shook her head. "I mean, Professor Pickard. He said he called the university. They're sending someone to get me."

Her eyes drifted toward the carnage. Neil's blood now looked like the splash of cranberry in her favorite alcoholic beverage.

She turned back to them. "We just have to wait until morning."

"I'm not staying here all night," Ally said. Tears flowed down her face. "No way."

Jill approached her. "We don't have a choice, Ally. We're safe here. The shark is in the ocean. Can't get to us."

The girl's eyes migrated toward the destruction, that incarnadine injection in the tranquil blue waters. "No way. I can't."

The muscles in Evan's face pulled taut. Facing the ocean, he gripped the balcony's railing and pulled himself onto his toes. Leaning over the railing, he screamed at the sea as if it had torn off his toenail.

Jill gawked at him. "Feel better, hotshot?"

Turning around, he sighed heavily. The kid looked wiped. His dreadlocks dangled in front of his pallid face. "No."

Jill could tell he wanted to cry along with Ally. He was doing a good job with his mask, but sooner or later, Jill thought, the mask would break and the tears would come like a long overdue rainstorm.

"How are you so calm?" Ally squealed at Jill. Her body vibrated with each sob.

"I'm real close to losing it," Jill said, lying. Fact was, the numbness she felt toward Pickard's untimely demise surprised herself. She was more worried about how she'd answer to what had happened here. She wondered if Pickard's wife would want to question her. "I don't know. I'm… okay. I'll be okay."

The girl glared at her as if there were a million questions bouncing between her ears and she couldn't decide which one to ask. She settled on, "Weren't you and the professor close?"

She thought back to all those times spent with Pickard. The weekend excursions. The breaks between classes wasted in the laboratory closet. Those long, sexually charged nights in his office. The mornings she awoke rolling across his empty bed. They came back to her in a rush, a collage of memories.

"We were once." She swallowed her creeping sadness, and they went down her throat like razor blades. "Look, I'm upset too. This should never have happened. We should have never come here. Neil should have handed the evidence over to the police. We are all dumb for letting him talk us into this. But we're here now and we're alive and we're going to stay that way." Her eyes found their way back to the Gulf. The blood had merged with the ocean water and made a tangerine pool around the fragments of fiberglass and splintered lumber. "Someone is coming to get us in the morning. After that, it will all be over. We'll put this horrible event behind us. Try to forget it ever happened. Move on."

"I'm calling someone now," Ally said, already thumbing around on her phone. "My father owns a commercial fishing company. I can have them send the coast guard."

"Ally," Evan said. "It's useless. You know cell phones don't work on this side of the island."

Confused, Jill shook her head. "I don't understand. I saw Neil using one. Remember? He called his wife."

Evan nodded. "Yeah, he had the satellite phone supplied by the university. Supposed to be used for emergency situations only, but, you know the professor and rules…"

Jill spread her arms apart. "I think this qualifies as an emergency situation, no?" She waited as if she expected him to answer. "Well, where is it?"

Evan looked over his shoulder.

Jill's shoulders went slack and she rolled her eyes. "Shit my pants."

"We're pretty much screwed."

Ally jumped in placed and held her hot pink phone in the air. "I think I got a signal!"

Evan furrowed his brow. Jill's heart leapt.

She put the phone on speaker so they could all listen to their rescuer's voice. Then an automated voice message interrupted the ringtone, crushing their high hopes: "Sorry," the robotic woman said courteously, "your call cannot be completed as dialed."

Ally almost tossed her phone over the balcony. Instead, she dropped to her knees and let out an exasperated scream. Jill knelt beside her, putting both hands on her shoulders. After a few minutes of consoling her, she helped the girl to her feet.

"We wait it out," Jill said with authority, like requesting license and registration information during a routine traffic stop. "Till morning."

"We could try the other side of the island," Evan said, the revelation causing his eyes to swell. "Rudders' must have a satellite phone! Or at least a way to communicate with the mainland!"

"Rudders'?" Not understanding, she shook her head. "What the hell is Rudders'?"

"It's a hotel. And a bar. I think. Don't know. Never been there."

"There's a hotel and a bar on this island and nobody told me?" Jill closed her eyes and scoffed. "Well, congratulations, the two of you have officially failed the friend test."

"They have to have a phone. Shit man, maybe even wifi!"

Ally perked up. "Let's go. Right now."

"Hold up, hold up, hold up," Jill said, raising a hand in the air.

"How far a walk is it to the other side of the island?"

"Island's not that big," Evan informed her. "Couple of hours? Don't really know."

Jill remained still. Deep down, she knew they should stay here and wait for rescue. Whomever Pickard sent would be expecting them here at the villa, not on the other side of the island. Besides, she didn't know what the tropical jungle had in store, what dangers they might run into. After what they'd seen, anything was possible.

This is a bad idea, she thought.

She was the queen of bad ideas and she wasn't ready to climb down from her throne quite yet.

Against her better judgment, she agreed with the students. "Okay. Let's take a walk."

20.

CJ sat exactly where Eddie had left him to go check on a "ruckus" happening out front, sitting with his back propped against the building, basking in the shade it provided. He sipped from a bottle of water, each gulp tasting like the elixir found in the fountain of youth. As Eddie hustled down the concrete pathway, CJ climbed the wall and managed to get himself to a standing position.

CJ noticed the grave look on Eddie's face immediately. "I'm okay," he assured the man, who stared at him with eyes too wide for their sockets. "Seriously," CJ said with confidence. "Just a little sore."

Eddie's expression didn't falter. "There's something out there. All the boats... they whole dock is gone."

CJ's nerves tingled with dread. "Oh shit. It," he gulped air, "it must have followed me."

"You know what it is?"

CJ shrugged. "It looks like a—"

"Shark?"

Nodding, CJ added, "A big one. With black skin. It... it killed my friend." Eyes stinging, he tried hard to cast aside the image of the shark's mouth closing on his friend's body. The image was seared into his brain. He couldn't shake it. "We found a bunch of bodies. It must have torn through a submarine or something. All this debris floated to the surface. Along with the dead."

Eddie looked away, as if something dangerous occupied his peripherals. "S.Q.U.I.D."

"I'm sorry? What?" CJ winced as the pain in the lower half of his body spiked. "Did you say *squid?*"

Eddie nodded. "Yes. There are these... *rumors.*"

"Rumors?"

"Of an underwater station somewhere out there in the Gulf. It's a tale fishermen who come here like to tell. My parents told me about it. Say that's all they talk about when they're all liquored up. Who saw what and so forth."

"That so?"

Eddie returned his gaze to CJ's eyes. "Yes. See, fishermen love to tell tall tales. There's not much else to talk about out at sea. Half the time—more than half the time—it's all bullshit. Stories to pass the time. I didn't believe this particular tale myself until I found something that washed ashore a few miles down the beach. It was one of those water-resistant wristbands. Read 'visitor.' Some guy's name was printed on it. Ronald something. I don't remember. But it had the acronym S.Q.U.I.D. printed next to it."

"Strange."

"Very."

"What do you think it means?"

Eddie flung his shoulders up. "Don't know. But I think the fishermen were right. There is something down there. Or *was*. Looks like whatever they were working on," he checked over his shoulder as if he expected eavesdroppers, then continued in a whisper, "escaped."

"What do you say we keep that hush-hush for now, Eddie." CJ looked past the bartender and saw the fishermen returning from the cliffside. Their faces were long, as if they were returning from a close family member's eulogy. "Are they going to be okay?"

Eddie turned. "Everything those men ever loved was on those boats."

"Damn." CJ squinted. "I mean, insurance will cover the damages, right?"

"Sure. But it'll take time. You know insurance companies. Savages they are." Eddie lit another smoke. "Be months before they get it all straightened out. They'll lose money for sure."

CJ changed the subject. "Eddie, we have to get off this island. Preferably by plane or helicopter."

Because I'm never going in the damned water again, he thought.

Eddie pondered this. "I can phone a hospital on the mainland. See if they can airlift you out. There's a landing pad on the roof."

"Thank God."

"I'll tell them to send authorities. I'll make up a story. Claim someone was murdered. They won't believe the truth over the phone, so I'll have to lie. But once they're here, once they see the destruction, they'll have to believe us. They'll have no choice."

CJ didn't think anyone would believe their giant, prehistoric shark story until they were up close and personal with the mammoth-sized beast. Then again, he hadn't seen what the creature did to the docks yet. Judging from the look on Eddie's face, he knew it was bad. The man looked haunted. His hands trembled and CJ figured it had nothing to do with the faint breeze blowing off the oceanfront.

Just then, a chill cut through CJ.

Eddie left to go make that phone call. He returned five minutes later with terrible news.

"They won't send anyone out until morning."

CJ glared at him with disbelief. "Did you tell them it was a goddamn emergency?"

"Sure did." Eddie shook his head. "They said a storm is coming. Bad one. They even named it." He looked skyward. In the distance, slate-gray clouds began feasting on the blue sky. Eddie placed his hands on his hips and kicked a pebble across the small patio. It skipped across the sand and into a patch of dune grass. "Shit!"

"It's okay. It's better than nothing." CJ didn't exactly believe that. Although he wouldn't consider himself in critical condition, he was still in a tremendous amount of pain. However, things had improved since Brinks and Gardner first discovered him. He had been more dehydrated than anything else. Although his knees felt like someone had taken a blowtorch to them and his body was cut and bleeding, and the sun blisters felt like he had spent the afternoon in Satan's chamber of torture, he otherwise felt okay. Pretty good, considering. He assumed his body had adapted to the pain, like the torment had taken a backseat to the nervous anxiety and overall ominous feelings about the island, about what could still happen here. He couldn't shake the feeling that something bad was on the horizon. It was like the storm clouds closing in on Key Water Island were harbingers of imminent death.

The parade of fishermen hauled themselves back into the bar, single file.

"Why don't we get you inside," Eddie told him, snapping CJ free from his dismal reverie. "We have air conditioning, and I don't know about you but I could sure as hell use a drink." He winked at him, lightly punched his arm. "First round is on me."

He nodded and followed Eddie around to the front of the hotel, where the entrance to the bar was located. A few fishermen were still filtering in, their heads tilted toward the ground. A few grumbled words of disbelief. CJ was right behind them, shocked by the recent events.

Eddie held the door open for him, ushering him inside with a friendly wave.

"You'll be safe in here," the bartender said. "No shark ever came to land."

CJ would soon find out how gravely mistaken Eddie was on both counts.

21.

Two hours after she and the others fled from the villa, Jill McCourty found herself bursting through the tropical shrubbery on the other side of the island. A long stretch of tall yellowed grass took up the space between the trees and a towering, mansion-like building that overlooked the Gulf.

Jill trekked on, toward the hotel, Ally jogging alongside her.

"Wait up!" Evan called.

"Hurry up," Jill said, not looking back.

"I'm tired. Can't we take a break?"

Ally smiled. Along the way, she had informed them of her high school cross country days, every accomplishment and accolade. Evan admitted to never running for recreation a day in his life. He did confess to smoking a lot of weed and partaking in the occasional acid trip throughout his high school career. Jill laughed it off and told him she was going to have the local authorities search his dorm once they were back on American soil. The empty threat silenced him, his face paling to a ghostly white. She told him she was joking, but he didn't seem convinced. He didn't speak another word until he whistled for the time out.

The girls ignored his request and continued briskly through the tall grass. Jill heard Evan rustling behind them, rushing to catch up. In the distance, the hotel became clearer. After a few minutes, she could read the sign printed in giant, neon-glow letters, unlit for the time of day: RUDDERS'. Below it, an invitation for rock-bottom beer specials.

She couldn't decide what she wanted more: a phone call to the mainland or a crisp, refreshing beer. She could almost taste the hoppy aroma biting her tongue. She yearned hard for both.

"Almost there," Jill said.

Behind her, Evan gasped for air. The way he was drawing in breath Jill thought something had punctured his lung. Hunched over, he produced an inhaler from his breast pocket. Placing the end of it in his mouth, he sucked hard. Evan repeated the process twice before catching the usual cadence of airflow.

Jill stopped, turned. "Jesus, kid. If you have asthma maybe you should lay off the bong."

Evan replied with a smile that said *yeah sure, lady, whatever you say.* He exhaled, a long relaxing release, and pocketed the small device. "Haven't gotten one that bad in years."

"Seriously, dude," Ally said, glancing at him over her shoulder. "You need to chill on the ganja."

He waved his hand in the air after the two women refocused their attention on the hotel.

About a hundred yards from their destination, the trio veered off their direct route and headed for the edge of the cliff. Dark clouds were assembling on the horizon, rolling toward Key Water Island. A storm was approaching.

Great, Jill thought. *Another problem we can add to the list.*

She wondered if this would affect their rescue. She prayed it wouldn't.

Ally stopped when she reached the cliff side, looked down and pointed. "Ho-lee shit."

Darting to her side, Jill followed the girl's finger. "Oh damn."

"What is it?" asked Evan, late to the party.

They didn't answer, mainly because they couldn't describe it with words. No quick response would do the scene justice.

The dock and the several boats that had been parked there rested in pieces, fragments of splintered wood and fiberglass. The debris floated back and forth on waves that were becoming more aggressive with each cycle. A strong gale blew wet mist off the rolling ocean water.

Jill immediately thought of Hurricane Katrina and the city of New Orleans. Living close to the aftermath at the time, she'd seen many pictures of obliterated houses floating in the Gulf; this was like that but only a fraction of the damage. Equally mind-blowing. She chalked that up to knowing what had caused the wreckage, and it surely wasn't the encroaching storm.

The Black Shark.

The monster that had snapped Pickard in half with one bite.

"Fuck," muttered Jill, not so silently. She turned and grabbed Evan and Ally by their arms and led them toward the hotel. "Let's check out Rudders'. I need a goddamn drink."

Like zombies, they shambled after her. Three minutes later

they were standing in front of the entrance. They glanced at each other, all wondering the same thing: what kind of people would they find inside? Furthermore, how accepting would they be to the truth?

Jill suspected they wouldn't believe a seventy-foot shark had rolled through and annihilated their precious possessions. She hoped to God they already knew.

"Don't mention the shark," Jill instructed them, pushing open the door.

They were greeted with turned heads and no smiles. It was as if they walked into the wrong funeral parlor viewing during the vigil. Jill almost backed herself out, but Evan and Ally blocked the exit. Ten seconds later they were old news, and the fishermen returned to their semi-private conversations and frosty glasses of ale.

Jill approached the bar cautiously, as if the floor tiles would give way to an infinite realm of endless black, and locked eyes on the long-haired bartender. He was buffing the bar top with a once-white-but-now-yellow rag when Jill reached the counter. He eyed her as if she'd come here with bad intentions.

"Help you?" he asked.

She couldn't help but feel like a criminal the way he was looking at her. "Please." She tried sounding pleasant rather than desperate, but failed. "My friends and I are trapped on this island, and we need to get off it. Now."

"Join the club, lady," he said coldly. The bartender, "Eddie" his name tag read, gestured to his patrons as if they were attractions at a freak show. "We're all stranded here."

A fisherman sporting a big, bushy beard the color of autumn leaves overheard their conversation and yelled, "A goddamn sea monster destroyed our boats!" He stood up from his chair and swayed on the balls of his feet.

The entire room erupted in a drunken, angry cheer.

"I say we start us a shark hunt!" another fisherman announced. He was sitting in the corner by himself, nursing a whole bottle of vodka. The way he wobbled sitting down made Jill wonder how he'd fare walking a straight line. None of the men in the bar looked in any condition to stand, let alone lead a shark hunt expedition.

"I want to hang the fucker's jaws on my mantle!" another man added.

"I love me some good shark meat!" added one more.

Another stood, wavering like a traffic light in a gale. He shouted, "Let's kill that sea monster!"

Another unified celebration.

After the applause died down, Ally stepped forward. "You've... you've all seen it?"

The auburn-bearded man nodded. "Destroyed that dock and our boats like they were glued together with popsicle sticks." Slowly, the man shook his head. "Ain't never seen a shark that big. Not ever. I know any better, I'd say that thing swam out of hell. Yes, ma'am."

Ally nodded. "It killed our professor. Bit him in half."

The room stood silent.

The auburn-bearded man finally asked, "Y'all from the university, I gather?"

Jill stepped in front of Ally. "Yes. We need to phone the mainland. Tell them what happened. I'm a police officer, a detective for Port—"

"We already called the mainland, lady," Eddie interrupted her from behind the bar, sounding somewhat crestfallen. "Storm is due to hit soon and they won't send anyone until morning."

Jill shook her head. "No, that's not good enough. We need someone now."

"Shark's in the water, missy. Ain't coming to land. We'll be fine until then. Meantime, we have air conditioning and plenty of beer to go around."

The room exploded with cries of happiness. Glasses clinked together. It was funny how much the very mention of alcohol could improve a situation.

Later, of course, they would wish they'd stayed sober.

Jill turned to the bar and drove her fists into the counter. The men stopped celebrating and gave her their full attention. The fury of a strange woman could not go ignored.

"I said it's not good enough," she barked. "And if you call me *missy* one more time, you'll be licking the shit out of your own asshole, got me?"

Eddie narrowed his eyes until no more white remained. A slow nod was his only response.

"Good." Jill stood up straight, her temper simmering. "Now, where's your phone?"

The bartender pointed to the corner of the bar.

Jill glanced over her shoulder. "Don't suppose you have some spare change?"

"For you," Eddie said, "I got all the change in the world."

22.

It was time.

The horizon had eaten part of the sun, halving it, allowing purple and tangerine smears to bleed through packs of puffy, gliding clouds. The temperature had dropped significantly. Above her, the winds kicked across the ocean, howling like sad wolves.

Below, she weaved through the waters, sensing the shore was near. Belly swollen with her unborn, nearly bursting now, she couldn't wait to rid herself of the burden. And the pain. Lugging the little ones around for the last several hours had been an arduous task. However, the end was near.

No, not near.

Here.

Ahead, the beach awaited. The shores loomed. Sharkwater Beach. She didn't know the humans called it that. To her, it was land. Soil. Rock. Not water. A foreign terrain she hadn't visited in over two thousand millennia, not since she escaped her home-world and found refuge in the deepest, darkest depths of the watery, alien planet. She wondered how it would feel on her skin, the sand, the earth. Her home-world had been mostly rock and dust and stone, but sand was similar to dust, and although the sensation was nothing but a distant memory, she could still feel the grit on her flesh. The prospect of being reacquainted delighted her.

Cruising through the shallows, surging toward the surface, she broke through the barrier and catapulted herself into the air. She sailed forth, her massive body completely leaving the water behind. She landed in the sand with a hard thud. The island seemed to shake around her. The trees whipped back and forth, and she realized it wasn't her impact that had caused their movement, but the prelude of the approaching weather. She skidded to a stop, several feet before where the tropical vegetation began and the beach ended.

Marooned, the Ocean Queen rolled on her side. She could feel her young bouncing in the womb, working their way toward the exit. A rush of adrenaline played with her nerves, nearly causing her whole system to crash. She held on. Consciousness dipped in and out. Then, an unimaginable pain settled in, filling every muscle with fire, like the pits of hell had opened up inside her. She opened her jaws and screamed, and the noise that emanated, carrying to all parts of the island, was a high-pitched whine foreign to Earth and the majority of the known universe. Had human beings been in the direct vicinity, their eardrums would have burst like hot lava from the tip an active volcano.

The stretch of flesh on her stomach undulated, moving like waves seeking a shore to crash down on. Wildly, the skin extended and sucked in, extended and sucked in. Her babies were ready, the birthing prepared to take place. This was it. All she needed to do was push.

Before her birthing hole could open and she could contract her muscles, squeeze with all her harnessed ferocity, a long gash opened up along her belly and a river of black, viscous fluids spilled out. A hot pain seared through her, infiltrating every organ. All at once she felt shock and agony, so overwhelming her brain felt like it had liquified from exposure to blue flames. She peeked at the damage and saw something slithering through her un-zippered flesh, something that looked oddly human.

An arm.

Covered and dripping in onyx syrup, the arm stretched out, grasping and pulling itself toward an earthly existence. The arm's muscles were impressively defined, shaped to perfection, Prometheus-like in tone and sculpture. At the end of its outstretched fingers protruded nails, catlike in the way they curved, semi-serrated, perfectly designed for tearing through flesh of all thicknesses. The Ocean Queen's rubber coat, along with the layers of blubber beneath it, was thicker than any other animal skin the new planet stocked; if it sliced through her epidermis so effortlessly, she could only imagine the damage they would cause human flesh.

A few more arms sliced through her, seeking escape from her crowded womb. Six limbs reached out of her eviscerated belly, searching for safe passage into the new world. They grabbed at the air wildly and clawed at the sand until they found traction, enough to drag themselves out. Next came their craniums, humanlike in design, but significantly otherworldly. Their dome-shaped skulls came to a point above the forehead, akin to shark fins. They had human ears, noses, and mouths, but their black, oily skin was completely alien. Their flesh sweat ichorous fluids. Pushing themselves out of their mother, they basked in the glow of the fading sun. They reared their leathery lips, exposing small, jagged rows of teeth that mirrored the jaws of the being that gave birth to them. A human tongue lolled over them, and their shark-like ivories sliced the surface of the pink muscle on contact. Standing, completely freed from their incubator, they stretched their intricately defined muscles and marveled over their bodies, examining each other like one would in the morning mirror. They faced each other, forming a triangle, hissed and squealed, communicating in their alien tongue. At their feet, lay the husk of the Ocean Queen, gutted, black liquid squirting from her children's exit and onto the sand. Once released, the blood crawled like an army of spiders, alive and seeking refuge from the fading light. The small, almost microscopic organisms needed darkness to thrive, as it was on their home planet. The three creatures hunched down and watched the black lake move toward the canopy of coconut trees. In minutes, every drop that had spilled from the Ocean Queen found its way into the shade. The organisms would wait in the jungle, gather its collective sense, then seek out other lifeforms for consumption.

The three newborn hunters weren't bothered by the fading sunlight. They could thank the humans for that; for their experiments; for injecting human DNA into the Ocean Queen during her time spent in hell.

The alien hunters gnawed at the air. They chirped to each other, wondering what would come next. One of them, one who had grown its eyes out the side of its head, resembling a hammerhead, careened its body and faced the Ocean Queen. Hammerhead stared into her cold, lifeless eyes. She had lost her life in the birthing process, an ending she hadn't exactly predicted but wasn't surprised by either.

Hammerhead dropped to its knees. Black slaver dangled from its lips. Opening its mouth wide as it would stretch, it leaned in and sank its teeth into its mother, ripping away a huge chunk of flesh and blubbery meat. It swallowed greedily. Before helping itself to seconds, it turned to its brothers.

The brother whose head came to a fin at the apex of its skull also sank to its knees. Fin-Head dropped its teeth on mother and began to consume, swallowing her flesh and the tough meat beneath. Inky soup poured down the carcass, running over Fin-Head's mouth. It felt a bit like eating itself, but the hunter didn't care—right now, food was food and it needed as much as it could find. Its stomach felt like a bottomless pit and it needed its mother's meat, just enough to fuel them until the next feast.

The third brother, whose misshapen head sported a single row of smaller fins, the alien-shark equivalent to the human Mohawk hairstyle, stumbled toward mother like a swaying drunk, lunged forward, and began to feast on its life giver. It chewed away huge chunks of obsidian flesh, digging for the thick, white meat beneath.

It fed.

They all fed.

They ate until their bellies were full. They ate until they could see mother's cartilage core.

Then the real hunt began.

Their mission of human eradication was underway.

* * *

Brinks sat up and faced the dying day. Majestic purple and traces of tangerine streaked through the clouds, giving him the finest sunset he'd ever seen. It was almost beautiful enough to heal his wounds and whisk away his pulsing pain. But nothing was that gorgeous. Clearly broken, his ribs ached. His lungs couldn't take in enough air, forcing short breaths. The restriction was uncomfortable, feeling like a ratchet strap had been tightened around his chest, though he'd survive. The bullet Gardner put through his shoulder had exited cleanly above his clavicle. Torment trolled the entrance and exit wounds, ebbing and surging, gone one second, killing him the next.

All in all, he considered himself lucky to be alive. Gardner was the best shot out of the three Goon Squad members. The way

Brinks saw it, he should have never crawled out of the ocean.

Gardner, he thought. *Back-stabbing son of a bitch.*

Plus, there was the shark. Why the beast hadn't gone after him left Brinks clueless.

After taking the bullet and jumping overboard, Brinks hit his head on something heavy, what he assumed was the dock, and then hit the water. He staved off unconsciousness, the invading bursts of white stars, for about thirty seconds as he frantically paddled for the shore. Then came the beast streaking through the shadows. The thing seemed blind to his presence and darted toward the docks.

At Gardner.

Somewhere along the way Brinks had stopped paying attention to what was happening behind him. When he reached the beach he didn't know if Gardner had survived the shark attack, but hoped to God the lengthy giant had eaten him slowly, chewed on every part of him while the fuck was still alive enough to feel it. Brinks tolerated a lot of things, but betrayal wasn't one of them.

Brinks surveyed the beach now. He didn't know where he was. Amidst the chaos of paddling to safety, he must have drifted down the shore because the docks and the cliff side hotel were nowhere in sight. It was doubtful the landmark was far from his current location. He wasn't in the water *that* long. But in which direction it rested, he didn't know. His internal compass was no longer working.

It hurt to stand, but not as much as he predicted. Blood dribbled from a few cuts on his arms and face. A lengthy gash had opened across his midsection. It burned from the salt. The surrounding skin was pink with agitation.

He'd survive. The cuts and bruises were the least of his worries. What troubled him was how he'd get off the island in one piece. Ronald sure as shit wasn't sending anyone. The boats were destroyed. A giant shark was circling the island. He couldn't swim his way home. He was at the mercy of the island and the beast that now controlled it.

I am totally fucked.

He made a quick decision about which direction to travel. As he moved down the beach, some alien sound made its way across the island. A high-pitched shriek that combined a bird squawking and a gust of wind howling across an open field. The peculiar cry lingered in the air, causing Brinks to stop dead in his tracks. The oddness of the sound stabbed his ears. He clapped his hands against the side of his head, protecting his hearing along with his sanity.

What the hell was that?

It sounded primitive. Prehistoric. A sound that did not belong on human ears.

Brinks squinted against the wind. His facial features pulled taut with concern.

As he waited for the horrible noise to abate, darkness swallowed up the remaining light, flooding the island with crawling shadows.

The sound soon died. He removed his hands from his ears, testing the silence. The island was eerily quiet. For several moments not even the wind spoke. It was as if the noise had frightened the island's essence into hiding. A moment later the wind returned. Sand granules kicked up off the beach. The clapping of small waves against the shore resumed. Brinks could hear the sound of his own stifled breathing again.

Whatever had made those strange sounds finally finished. He needed to move. Nightfall had arrived. His only light source came from above, that hanging white orb in the sky. He'd stick to the beach and let the stars point him north. He didn't want any part of what might be inhabiting the center of the island. Didn't want any part of whatever made that terrible noise.

All he wanted was off this hell hole.

23.

"Sleep?" the frantic girl asked. "You expect me to sleep in this dump!"

Until that moment Jill thought Ally was a down-to-earth kind of girl, someone she identified with in her previous life. In an ordinary social environment, she might have even considered being friends with her despite the fact Jill never gelled with other women. Ally seemed sharp, perhaps too bubbly, too much valley girl in her blood, but otherwise nice, caring, and honest. There had been a sweet innocence to her. Not jaded and certainly not the my-daddy's-super-rich-bitch-mode that she currently displayed.

"Ally," Jill said, "help will be here soon."

"I can call my father." She was sitting on the edge of the twin bed, the one she had claimed was infested with bugs. "He'll have someone here within the hour. Storm or no storm."

Staring up at the water-stained ceiling tiles, Jill closed her eyes and cleared away all the nasty words that populated in her verbal queue. "Ally, I called my lieutenant. If they could send someone earlier, they would. There's a bad storm just off the coast. It's already in progress. And from the looks of it, it's coming toward us. It's too dangerous to fly. Trust me. I want off this island just as much as you do."

"Our professor is dead!" Her shrill voice sliced through Jill's nerves. *"Neil is dead!"*

"I understand," she said through her teeth. "You're upset. We all are." She turned and nodded at Evan who hung near the doorway. "Isn't that right, Evan?"

Evan nodded, keeping his eyes trained on the floor.

Jill rubbed the girl's shoulder. "The storm is due to pass during the night. The second it ends, they'll shoot someone out here." She brushed a rogue hair away from Ally's face. "I promise. It's going to be okay."

"You don't care," Ally said, tears brimming on her eyelids. "You don't care he's gone."

Sighing, Jill took up the space next to her. "Of course I do. Neil and I were close once."

"You mean, you two were fucking." It wasn't a question.

Jill winced, the statement hitting her like a slap. "Yes. Yes, we were. But it was more complicated than that."

"You loved him."

Jill took a moment before confirming what Ally already knew. "Yes. Yes, I did."

Evan raised his forefinger. "I'm going downstairs to grab a beer. Maybe get some fresh air. All this girl talk is making me sick."

The girls elected to ignore his exit, keeping the conversation going without missing a beat.

"He left you," said Ally.

"Yes." Jill hung her head. "I caught him with... with someone else."

Ally's lips cracked. Jill saw the girl wanted to smile out of her peripherals.

"Typical Neil." Ally sniffled. Her mouth moved in a way that suggested she was recalling fond memories. "He was what you might call a 'player.'"

"Oh yeah. Big time." It wasn't easy, but she managed to control the images threatening to take over her thoughts. Images of Pickard. What he looked like in bed. On top of her. Thrusting. "Yeah, and I knew it, too. He had a reputation. Sleeping with other professors. Not students. No way. Nothing like that. I thought I was the first. I thought I was special. I thought the feelings we shared were deeper." She looked over at Ally. "I thought I was different."

Ally understood. She nodded. "Why did you come back to Sharkwater Beach?"

Jill thought carefully. She wasn't completely sure she knew the truth herself. The last twenty-four had been a whirlwind of confusion. She settled on, "It's complicated."

Ally glared at her through glassy eyes. "Tell me."

Jill threw herself back, sprawling on the bug-infested comforter. She stared up as if the answer to Ally's question was etched on the ceiling tiles. She gave herself thirty seconds to sift through the past, reviewing her mistakes, analyzing every decision, combing over the Jill she was now, how her relationship with Pickard had shaped her into the woman she'd become. How it murdered the girl she once was.

"I guess…" A false start. "Fuck, Ally." Then it all came out. "I guess a part of me thought Neil was still interested. God, I've become such a miserable bitch over the last few years. I thought I could… If I saw him again and somehow confronted the past, I thought I could go back to being me, the girl I was in college. Happy. Normal. Sane. *Fuck.*"

"Did it work?"

"Not really." Jill closed her eyes. "I never knew he married," she added. "Had I known, I would have jammed that shark tooth right up his asshole."

Ally managed a small grin. "Did you know he was banging Monica?"

Jill suspected Neil was still up to his old tricks. Especially after she saw what happened on the boat, the moments leading up to their untimely demise. "No. I didn't. Fact is, I didn't know anything. I should have been smart. I should never have answered his call. I wouldn't fucking be here. I'd be continuing to live out my shitty, miserable existence. Alone." She sat and swallowed a lump. "I guess being alone isn't all that bad. There's a lot less pain when you're alone."

"Yeah. There is."

"Fuck."

"But at least you know now." Ally rested her head on Jill's shoulder. "At least you know that the professor was an asshole who'd never change. That has to feel good. Somewhat comforting?"

Jill recalled the image of Pickard meeting the black shark's jaws. The way his body bent when the unearthly bear trap of a mouth came down on him.

"Yeah. Sort of." She slapped Ally's leg. "I'll get over it. What's that adage? Time heals all wounds?"

"Yeah."

"Yeah, I like that." Jill blinked away tears. "This is going to sound harsh, but I'm almost relieved he's gone."

Ally glared at her.

"Not, like, happy. I won't be doing the salsa on his grave, or anything like that. Fuck, Ally, I'm not that big of a bitch." She drew a long deep breath and let it out just as slowly. "Just… relieved. I won't have to wonder anymore. I won't have to imagine a world where we're together and happy, because it can no longer happen." Jill wrinkled her nose. "Fuck, that makes me a bad person, doesn't it?"

Squinting, Ally replied, "It's very dark, but no. I don't think you're a bad person." She swallowed tears. "Besides, I guess looking back, Professor Pickard wasn't the nicest person. I mean, to do that to his wife…"

"Oh yeah. Dude was a major dick."

Ally nodded. "Maybe we should talk about something else."

"Totally. Let's promise to not mention the prick's name ever again. Not until we're safe. On the mainland."

"Promise."

They shook their pinky fingers on it.

"How are you holding up otherwise?" Jill asked.

Ally shrugged. "Feeling anxious. I have anxiety issues. I have a prescription for it, but I left it in my dorm. Hardly ever need it."

"Well, just think happy thoughts. All we have to do is survive the bed bugs and tomorrow morning we're off this shithole."

"Yeah, I know. I just get the feeling something bad is going to happen." She shivered. "Don't you feel it? It's like… in the air or something."

Jill offered her a pained smile, a poor attempt at hiding how similar she felt. "No," she lied. "No, we're going to be just fine. Don't worry about a thing." The next smile seemed more genuine, although she feared Ally saw right through it. She might have acted as if her head was above the clouds, but she wasn't brainless. Far from it. "I'm a cop, remember? I have, like, superpowers. I can usually tell when something bad is going to happen."

"Did you bring your gun?"

A strange question. The sea monster they'd seen was in the water. Their ride would come by air. They were safe, no firearm needed. "Yes. It's in my bag." The bag in question rested on the other bed.

"Can you… keep it close?"

Dropping her smile, Jill asked, "Ally, what in God's name do you think is going to happen?"

Her lips trembled. "Something *horrible.*"

And with that, a throat-ripping scream bellowed from somewhere close. Below them. Outdoors. Down by the beach. A man's voice. Sheer horror.

Color drained from Ally's face, giving her the complexion of an emaciated vampire. Both women immediately recognized the source of the scream.

It was Evan.

24.

Brinks followed the beach until he came across some wreckage that had washed ashore. The debris contained the following: jagged deck boards; splintered fiberglass; a Whaler's steering wheel; an emergency medical kit sans the medical supplies; a pile of broken fishing poles; spools upon spools of tangled fishing wire; a radio antenna; and Gardner's bloody arm from the elbow down.

He knew the arm had been Gardner's because of the small tattoo of his estranged daughter's birthdate on his wrist. Seeing the arm filled him with satisfaction. It wasn't a proud moment, but the son of a bitch had tried to kill him, so *fuck him.* If the saddle was on the other horse, Gardner would have harnessed the same emotions.

Brinks wondered if Hanson had been in on it, and not for the first time during his walk. Given how the two were close, it was a reasonable notion, though getting blown to bits probably wasn't on the pair's agenda. Neither was getting eaten by a giant shark.

I'll ask that fat motherfucker Ronald when I have my hands around his fucking neck, Brinks said to himself. Imagining that scenario filled his insides with fire, a rage that burned on for several minutes until the hotel and cliff came into view, the Rudders' marquee glowing brightly in the dark sky.

As he stumbled toward it, he wondered what condition the kid was in. Although he was confident he'd survive, the sun poisoning hadn't looked good. He wondered if the island rednecks were able to get him antibiotics. He doubted the dingy hotel was equipped for such. Odds were, the kid was hurting and on the brink of some serious medical complications.

He began to ascend the hill when something stirred to his right. It sounded like leafy foliage spreading apart and footsteps landing on dead, crunchy leaves. With his adrenaline already at its peak and his nerves running uncomfortably numb, Brinks spun so quickly he almost knocked himself over. His hands were balled into fists, ready to strike the first thing that appeared before him.

"Whoa!" yelled a young kid sporting a wiry mane of

dreadlocks. He held a bottle of light beer out like a dagger. "I come in peace, dude!"

Brinks relaxed, breathing a deep sigh of relief. "What the hell, kid?" He combed him over with his eyes. The kid looked no older than twenty-one. He wore glasses that reflected the moonlight, and his blue T-shirt had a surfing company's yellow logo printed on the chest. His swim trunks looked wet with something and when the wind changed direction, Brinks knew exactly what. "What are you doing out here?"

"That's a long story, mister," Evan said, a slight slur accompanying his words. He peered over his shoulder, seeming to not want the tropical foliage behind him to hear. "Let's see. I was on a school trip. My teacher got eaten by a giant mega shark." Evan giggled like a ticklish child. "Fucking nuts, right? I hardly believe it myself."

Brinks squinted at the stoner. "You're drunk."

Evan gave him a good old-fashioned raspberry. "Psssh. You're drunk."

"And you have the humor of a three-year-old. Great." Brinks shook his head. "Why is this island full of needy nerds and not hot babes, that's what I want to know."

Swaying on his heels, Evan writhed his lips. "You're nerdy, man. Whatever. Hey look. What are *you* doing out here? You don't look like a fisherman. Are those cuts on your—"

Brinks felt his face ignite. "Shut up! Who I am is not important. What *is* important is how we're getting off this island."

"Okay, *Mr. Serious.*"

Brinks hobbled over to him, immediately going for the smart mouth's throat. He gripped the stoner's esophagus, sinking his fingers into the muscle, and snarled. "Listen, you shit."

"It's Evan," he rasped. Barely enough air for him to breathe escaped his windpipe.

"Evan. I'll make you a deal. My leg hurts like a sonuvabitch. Help me up the hill and I'll buy you another beer." He loosened his grip so the kid could speak clearly. "Also, I won't break your teeth."

"More beer *annnnd* I get to keep my teeth? Deal."

"Good." He let go. "First let me rest. I've had a day you

wouldn't believe."

"Tell me about it." Evan rubbed his throat. "Dude, you have the grip of a Pterodactyl."

"Help me." Brinks bent down. Evan grabbed one of his arms and helped lower him to the sand. "Back is fucked up, too."

"It's probably because you're really old. Are those liver spots on your face or freckles. It's dark. I can't tell."

Brinks glared at him. "Have you ever been a fight, kid?"

"No, sir."

"Well, keep talking. Tonight might bring your first."

Something darted down the beach, cutting through the darkness. The moonlight barely picked up its image as it galloped on two legs, crouching down as if it could easily run on all fours, streaking across the beach with the swiftness of a small fox. A tail whipped back and forth, slicing through the air, approximately eight feet long. The end of the tail sported a two-lobed fin, mimicking that of a shark. A second later, the entire length of the unknown creature was lost when it ducked into a cluster of tropical trees.

"What the—" Evan looked down at Brinks. "Did you see that?"

Brinks tried to follow where the kid had been looking. Because of the darkness and the shadows the island wore, Brinks couldn't secure a good look. There had been something moving swiftly in the dark, yes—but what, he didn't know.

Something told him not to stick around to find out.

"Help me up," Brinks said, extending his hand to Evan.

Evan pulled him to his feet. "What are we doing?"

"I think we should get moving."

"Nah, man. Fuck that!" The kid cocked his head back and drained what remained of the bottle. He tossed the empty into the exotic, colorful underbrush. Ferns and tropical flowers swallowed the glass object, the island's darkness concealing it for the rest of eternity. "If someone is out there messing with us, I want to know!"

Brinks gritted his teeth. "Kid. Now isn't the time to see how big your balls are. Let's go. Right fucking now." His sixth sense kicked in, funneling adrenaline throughout his system. His senses told him to bolt faster than a rabbit in a wolf den. "You're shit-faced and if there is something out there—something dangerous—then you probably shouldn't be near it. And since I'm hardly a hundred percent, neither should I."

In that moment the rain came. The distant patter of droplets hitting the island's vegetation quickly became not-so-far away. The ordinarily-soothing sounds of nature filled their ears. A grumble of thunder and a quick flash lightning buddied with the tropical shower.

"I don't give a fuck!" Evan said, puffing his chest out. Two beers had given him the courage of a king lion. "I want to—"

His words were cut off by vicious snarls. The same figure that had streaked through the dark reappeared, jumping out from the nearby foliage and onto Evan's chest, forcing him to the ground. Brinks watched in horror as the beast opened its mouth and displayed three sets of needle-like teeth. Inky slobber dripped down its chin as it hissed like an enraged feline. The oil-like substance sputtered from the back of its throat, speckling Evan's face. The kid screamed like someone cut off his hand with a hatchet. He shrieked and shrieked until his voice went raw and gave out.

The beast's head jerked forward and stretched its jaws wide. Evan's head disappeared into the creature's mouth. The teeth sank into his flesh, immediately drawing rivulets of blood. With a quick twist, the monster snapped Evan's neck, the sound like a whole roll of bubble wrap getting popped at once temporarily silencing the storm. The creature pitched its head back, peeling away scraps of Evan's face with its teeth. Strips of the kid's face dangled off its chin like lettuce. Fluids poured over the beast's chin and down its chest, a bib of blood and black matter.

Brinks crab-walked away, slowly, careful not to draw attention to himself. While trying to make a quiet escape, he examined the creature, taking special notice of its human qualities. Besides the long tail, the pencil-like nails, the rows of teeth, and the crescent fin resting atop its head, the thing resembled something oddly human. It walked on two legs. Had two arms. A face. A body. Muscles. Opposable thumbs.

But human?

Brinks didn't think so.

Moonlight gleamed off its sweaty, rubberlike skin. It chewed on the meat it had stripped from Evan's face, paying Brinks no mind. Brinks watched the kid's chest rise and fall. Rise and fall. He was alive, opting for silence. Playing dead. Or maybe he passed out. Brinks couldn't tell. After the creature finished the appetizer, it dug into Evan's stomach, searching for the main course. With its talon-like nails the abomination un-zippered Evan's midsection, drawing a single nail down from his chest to his pubic bone. Viscera and ropey sections of intestines teemed out of the laceration, spilling like cotton fluff from an old Teddy Bear onto the sandy ground below. Fin-Head hungrily shoveled the offering into his mouth, swallowing without taking a single breath.

Brinks nearly shit himself when two more of the creatures darted out from the jungle, joining their brother's meal. Fin-Head allowed them to eat, but Brinks got the sense it wanted to let the others know the kill belonged to him, and they were only eating because he allowed it. Fin-Head gave them warning bites on their necks, which weren't received warmly. The creatures hissed at each other, and for a brief moment Brinks wondered if the monsters would tear into each other, making his escape a lot less harrowing.

Actually, he prayed for it.

Let them kill each other. Please God, let them rip each other to pieces.

Brinks rose to his feet. He'd distanced himself twenty yards from the carnage. While the three beasts were nipping at each other and squawking in their alien tongues, Brinks turned and booked it down the beach, fear acting as a natural painkiller. The terror spread down his spine and leaked into his limbs, numbing everything. He couldn't feel an ounce of hurt.

To help motivate himself, he imagined the creatures on his heels, snarling like rabid dogs. A few hundred feet and he was convinced his imagination and reality had merged, that the damned things *were* directly behind him. He sensed hot breath on his neck. That rotten-ocean stink found his nostrils. A hellish stampede pounded in his ears. He felt the wind from their

whipping tails brush his ear.
Maybe they were behind him after all.
He didn't look back.
He ran.

25.

CJ's knee throbbed. Even sitting there, nursing his bottle of Dos Equis, the pain in his lower extremities pulsed and burned, sending waves of agony throughout his entire body. The blisters were no picnic either; they still hurt like little gateways to hell had opened on his flesh. Burned as if the sun were projecting death rays on him. All he wanted to do was crawl up into a ball and sleep for fifteen hours straight. The alcohol wasn't helping with the pain or the creeping memories of Duke, but who was he to turn down free drinks?

Duke.

He eyed the empty chair across from him, wishing his friend was there. Duke would know how to lighten the mood with a cheesy joke. Even if the jokes were trash, the two could still find humor in them.

Duke.

CJ suddenly wished the shark had taken him and spared his friend. Duke didn't deserve to die. Neither did he, but out of the pair, Duke had the more promising future. He had a chance with his comedy—a microscopic, snowball's-chance-in-hell chance, but a chance nonetheless. CJ's chances of glory ended when the doctor told him the damage to his knee would forever sideline his football career. Duke had his voice. His talent. His knack.

Now he was gone.

CJ kept hoping this was all a bad dream, that the front door to Rudders' would swing open and he'd turn to see Duke strolling through the lounge, pointing his finger at his best friend with one hand, pumping his fist with the other. He waited, but the moment never came.

Eddie checked in on him every twenty minutes or so. His generosity and concern weren't enough to pull CJ out of his funk. The next time he approached him with two mugs of Dos Equis, CJ waved him off.

"I think I'm done," he told him.

"Nonsense," Eddie replied, setting the mugs down. "I can tell when a man needs a drink, and you, sir, need a goddamn drink."

"What happened to your sobriety?"

Eddie had told him how he ended up tending bar at his folks' place, the abridged version.

"Shit, kid." He pointed to the two mugs, overflowing with foam. "They're both for you. If I'm going to piss away my sobriety, it won't be on beer."

Just as CJ was going to open his mouth to tell Eddie he'd pass on the generous offer and ask to be shown to his room, the front door swung open and slammed against the wall.

Every head in the room turned toward the entrance. CJ was the first, hoping his vision came true, that Duke had come back.

Although he recognized the intruder's face, it wasn't Duke's.

The men in the room stood, also recognizing the man. It was the stranger who tried stealing one of their boats.

"There's something out there," the man—Brinks, CJ remembered—said gruffly.

The fishermen didn't react. They stared at the stranger with uncertainty, examining the fear printed on his face, deciding whether his claim should be taken seriously.

"Monsters," Brinks clarified. "Three of them. Maybe more. I don't know, I... I ran." He was shaking violently. Losing his footing, he stumbled forward, then caught himself on a nearby table. The burly fisherman on his left watched as if he hoped Brinks ended up on the floor. "We're not safe here."

One fisherman stepped forward. The man with the red beard asked, "What do you mean, monsters?" His eyes were so slim that CJ couldn't see the white around his irises anymore. His face ruddied with anger. "Do you take us for fools?"

Brinks shook his head furiously. "No, no, no. I'm not messing around. That kid—"

Just then, two women entered the bar area via the staircase in the far corner of the room. Now every head turned toward them.

"Has anyone seen Evan?" the younger of the two asked. CJ remembered she had introduced herself as Ally. She seemed bubbly by nature, but current events had seemed to squash her peppy attitude. She couldn't hide the fear in her voice. "We thought we heard him—"

"Scream?" Brinks asked.

The two women fixed their gaze on the stranger.

"I saw him," Brinks said. "The monsters. They... they *got him.*"

The room shifted their attention back on the stranger.

Brinks was breathing heavily. He clutched his chest. CJ thought the man was a few seconds away from cardiac arrest.

"The monsters," Brinks repeated. "They got him. Tore him to shreds."

Before anyone wrote him off as a bonafide nut-job, a loud, ear-piercing screech tore through the night. It sounded like a whistling tea kettle, only decibels louder. Next came feral snarls—right outside the door.

Brinks ducked down and hid behind the table as if the creatures could see through walls. CJ eyed him suspiciously. This was hardly the same man who had rescued him earlier that day, who had helped lug him halfway across the island. This was a man on the verge of losing his sanity. He pranced around the table like the devil himself were knocking on the door to Rudders'.

Footfalls on the driftwood deck stopped. The sound of creaking lumber died off, too. A shadow blocked the moonlight from creeping under the door.

Someone was outside.

Something.

Monsters.

Three of them.

A chill curled around the top of CJ's spine and snaked its way down.

No one in the bar moved. Monsters or not, the shrill noise they had heard was not something that inspired much hope. CJ figured, in a world where giant black sharks were not mere figments of one's imagination, anything was possible.

Especially monsters.

After a few minutes of quiet, the red-bearded fisherman stormed toward the front door. He shouted, "Fuck this!" as he puffed out his chest and waved his arms to the rhythm of his march. He was the tallest man in the room by at least three inches. CJ got the sense he wasn't a man who'd back down from confrontation by the way he hustled, no hesitation breaking his stride.

Before anyone could voice their objection, Red Beard ripped open the door. A lanky figure, at least nine-feet tall, filled up the doorway, crouching to fit, to look its aggressor in the eyes before it struck to kill.

Baring rows of sharp, saw-like teeth—impossibly white—it swiped its talon-esque fingers across Red Beard's throat. An arterial spray of crimson gushed from the dark furrow, showering the creature in human blood. The humanoid monster filled its mouth with red like a parched prisoner escaping beneath rainy skies.

Screams and cries of shock and panic filled the room. The fishermen abandoned their libations and searched for the nearest exit. For some, that meant the windows. Others found the stairs. A door next to the bar that led to a small kitchen. Some hurled themselves at the wall, hoping the plywood would give way and allow them access to the world outside. The safe world, a world where tall black creatures with the features of both human and shark could not trespass.

But that wasn't the case.

As Red Beard's throat emptied in a surge of spurting blood, the creature who had lacerated him, the one with a single fin protruding from the top of its skull, sunk its jagged mouth into the soft tissue between the man's neck and shoulder. With savage force, the monster flung its head back, tearing away a mouthful of the fisherman's meat. It chewed vigorously. As it swallowed, it scanned the room for its next victim. There were many options. Locking eyes with a fisherman who smelled like fresh ocean spray, it sprang forward and mounted its target. The two bodies went to the floor with a heavy thud, scattering nearby chairs. The man's shrieks and cries for help intensified when Fin-Head dragged its claws down his face, disfiguring the man, painting his features red with blood in one violent rake. Next, the creature dug its hooks into the man's throat, ripping free his vocal cords. Shoveling more gore into its mouth, Fin-Head's eyes swept across the pandemonium.

A few of the fishermen managed to escape. They bustled through the front door. Outside, more screams as the escapees met with the other members of Fin-Head's killing crew. A minute later, Hammerhead's face appeared in the window, his maw dripping with fisherman blood. His eyes were as black as the galactic expanse above.

CJ's vision spun. As he watched the gory violence unfold, he thought that this was it. He was gonna die, here, drunk, already hurting both emotionally and physically. He was going to become disemboweled by a monster that shouldn't exist. He was going—

A hand clamped down on his shoulder. He almost emptied his bladder. Gasping, he turned to see who had interrupted his final thoughts.

Eddie.

He looked as frightened as CJ felt.

"Come on," Eddie said, pulling him out of his chair. He dragged CJ toward the stairs, the only safe place that wasn't becoming bottlenecked with escapees.

The sickening sounds of men watching their own mutilations became muted as he followed Eddie and the others upstairs.

* * *

Four fishermen made it outside and were able to skip past the two creatures as they snacked on two fresh, screaming meals. They made it about a hundred feet from Rudders' when they stopped and looked back. The creatures weren't following them. They were safe.

For the time being.

One of them suggested they scatter, meet up later on the other side of the island. The creatures couldn't follow all of them. Could they?

Unless there was more of them, one suggested.

They ignored that logic. Each survivor picked a different point on the compass and darted off in that direction, promising they wouldn't look back until they were free and clear from any and all chaos.

The man who had taken the north route died before he could total a hundred feet. Mohawk sniffed him out and hunted him down like a fox chasing a rabbit with a broken leg. The man felt something land on his back. The next thing he knew was pain, a lot of it, coursing through his veins like tainted drugs. Before the lights went out, he listened to the audible break of Mohawk snapping his neck. It sounded like lightning splitting an aged tree.

After the kill, Mohawk traveled west. The man who went was extraordinarily large, looking like a fisherman who ate more than he caught. He had no business sprinting through the dark. No business other than lugging aboard crab traps and nets full of shrimp. Mohawk caught up with him in almost no time. He spilled his intestines with one ferocious slice across his midsection. The messy assemblage of organs tumbled free to the ground like mishandled groceries.

The man who went east got his turn minutes later. Mohawk ripped the man's arms from their sockets, tossing them into the veritable darkness that enclosed Key Water Island. Blood sputtered from the fresh cavities. Mohawk showered in the scarlet drizzle, drinking from the tap, savoring each delicious drop.

At last came the man who drew south. South was the quickest of the four survivors, but still no match for Mohawk's superior speed. South almost made it to the jungle, which would have served him well, at least for a little while. He made the decision to hide and wait out the carnage. Morning would come and he could plan his escape then. He was about to dive into a bush and put his solid plan into action when something sharp entered him from behind and appeared before him, just below where his chin hit his chest when he looked down. He glanced at the object, and in the time it took for him to die he realized he was seeing his own heart, beating in the palm of an alien, black hand.

Back inside Rudders', the malice moved forward. Fin-Head and Hammerhead cleared the room and the immediate area outside. The bar floor looked like an episode of *Hoarders* if the focus family was a gang of serial murderers who liked to dissect their victims. Appendages and puddles of blood covered the floor, leaving very little foot space. Rivers of red flowed into small lakes of dark crimson. Splashes of gore painted the walls. Scarlet puddles stretched across the tables that once housed tall glasses of beer and plates of finger food. The entire room reeked of death and blood and vomit, thick with the overpowering sense of miasma. There were so many body parts strewn about, no one— not even a veteran medical examiner—would be able to decipher what belonged to whom; a true smorgasbord of human anatomy.

Hammerhead finished his meal, raising his bloody maw from an eviscerated fisherman. The room was eerily quiet and still. Not a single human remained alive.

Fin-Head also abandoned his current snack. His face was smeared with dark red, but the gore looked black against its alien skin.

They spoke telepathically.

Mohawk snuck in through the front door, his entire body bathed in human blood.

The three of them sniffed the air, picking up a sweet, intoxicating scent.

Survivors.

There was more work to do.

26.

Jill placed her eye against the crack between the door and its jamb, and peered down the hallway. It looked unoccupied from her vantage point, free from whatever the hell had raided the bar and shredded its patrons apart, so she pushed the door wide open. The entire length of the hall was indeed vacant.

Whispers were sent over her shoulder, urging her to utilize caution.

She waved the voices down.

Creeping forth, she left the stairwell and entered the hallway. No one followed her at first, fear holding them back. Jill had heard their concerns, that maybe the monsters had taken the *other* stairwell, and that the two parties would intersect on one of the hotel's floor. But Jill had a better idea: "We'll hide in one of the rooms on the top floor," she had told them, "and we'll get to the roof once the storm passes. Someone will be coming first thing in the morning. Then we're out of here." She neglected to tell them that someone would be expecting them on the opposite end of the island, but she figured she had time to work out the fine details.

She managed about ten feet before looking over her shoulder and realizing she was the only one venturing out of the stairwell. She waved them on.

Ally came first, crouching so low she was practically on all fours. The thin carpet under their feet didn't do much to deaden the sound of their footsteps. Jill figured crouching did nothing except exert unnecessary energy, so she rose up and suggested the others do the same silently by wagging her fingers.

Eddie the bartender and CJ came next, Brinks following closely behind. Out of the five of them, it was a toss-up between who looked worse: Brinks or CJ. Brinks's bullet wound was leaking thick, yellowish fluids. The surrounding flesh was eggplant purple. His clothes were ripped and torn, revealing deep cuts and blackened bruises. His face was pallid, clammy. His eyes seemed to bounce in every direction, unable to focus clearly on the task at hand. CJ was in better shape mentally, more aware of his surroundings, more focused. Even though his face and arms were the color of boiled lobster, he remained unrestricted by his harmful exposure to the sun. He walked behind Eddie, following him down the hall.

They managed about ten paces when Brinks cried out and dropped to the floor, clutching his infected wound.

The four other survivors turned to him.

"I'm done," he said hoarsely. He writhed on the carpet, face up. When the ebbing pain left his shoulder, he reached for the two knives on his belt. After he freed them from their hilts, he tossed one to Eddie; the other he kept for himself. "Stick a fork in me."

Jill nodded. "Let's go."

"Hey," CJ said. "We can't just leave him."

Jill kept walking. "Then stay with him. I don't give a shit."

Ally followed her.

CJ turned back to Brinks.

Brinks glared at the kid. "I left you to die. You can do the same for me."

The kid shook his head. "No, I can't."

Eddie bent down and scooped up the knife.

"I'm not asking you, kid," Brinks growled. "I'm telling you. I'll only hold you fuckers back. I'm as good as dead. A walking corpse. I can feel the infection working into my bloodstream. I can't wait until morning. I'll be dead by then."

CJ remained still.

Brinks continued: "Best I can do is slow those fuckers down. Give you all the best chance to reach the roof."

Somewhere below, the creatures chittered with delight.

Down the hall, Jill slipped her keycard into the acceptor. "I'll be right back," she told the rest of the group before dipping inside the room.

While Jill retrieved her firearm, Brinks was still convincing Eddie and CJ to go on without him.

"Nothing you can do, kid," Brinks reassured him.

"Come on, man," Eddie said, tugging on CJ's arm. "Let's go. The douche wants us to let him die, let him die."

Brinks nodded in agreement. He glanced down at the hunting knife in his hand, a contemplative look that suggested he wanted to use it on his own throat.

CJ turned around and headed down the hall as Jill emerged from her room, holding her gun with both hands.

"Ready?" she asked the group, but no one responded. "Okay then. You?" She nodded at Eddie. "Where's the roof hatch?"

Eddie shrugged. "The top floor."

"What floor are we on?"

"One floor away."

"Okay. Let's head back to the stairwell. We have to move quickly."

"What about the storm?" CJ asked.

"What about it?"

CJ's eye migrated upward. "You said someone would get us in the morning. It's going to storm until then. You expect us to wait it out on the roof? The entire night?"

"We can't use the roof," Ally said, tears spilling over her eyes. "They'll get us."

Jill looked over her shoulder. "Ally, it's our only way out. Remember, Pickard sent for a helicopter. Someone from the university will be here in the morning. We're going to have to wait it out. Storm or no storm, we have no choice."

"No one is coming," Ally said.

Jill turned to her. "What do you mean?"

As tears poured down her face, the girl's eyes darted back and forth nervously. "They're coming to Sharkwater Beach, not here."

Jill rolled her eyes. "Honey, we'll flag them down. The island isn't that big. They'll see us." Her voice lacked confidence, and the rest of the group picked up on it. Especially Ally. "They have to. They won't leave without us."

"Sharkwater Beach," Ally repeated softly. "Sharkwater Beach." Louder the second time. Then, she screamed, "Sharkwater Beach!"

"Ally," Jill said in her best calming voice. "You need to be quiet. They'll hear us."

Frantically, Ally kept shouting, "Sharkwater Beach! Sharkwater Beach! Sharkwater—"

"Shut up, you bitch!" Eddie shouted, taking the knife Brinks had given him and jamming into the girl's neck. A spurt of blood erupted from the puncture, splashing across Eddie's face. Shocked by his own mindless reaction, he backed away until his spine knocked against the wall. As if he had been shot in a Tarantino movie, he slid down until he was squatting on the floor. He opened and closed his mouth as if he were biting air, producing no words. He wiped away the wet, sticky feeling on his face and shrieked when his palm came away covered with the girl's blood.

Ally clapped her hand over the knife wound. Blood jetted through her fingers. Her eyes rolled underneath her eyelids. She fell forward into Jill's waiting arms. For a minute she remained there, trembling as if she were locked inside a freezer box.

And then she went rigid—dead.

"What the fuck did you do?" Jill asked, her voice a deep growl. She was clutching the girl tightly against her chest, ignoring the stream of blood that leaked down her clothes. "What the fuck did you do?"

"I didn't..." Eddie's eyes were glassy with regret. His lips quivered. Sniffling, he covered his eyes with his palms, rubbing them, not realizing he was painting his face with the girl's sanguine fluids. "Christ, I didn't mean to. She was—she was talking... Th-the creatures, th-they were gonna hear her."

No one spoke. Brinks lowered his gaze to his own death wound. CJ eyed the ceiling. Jill glared at him, the muscles in her cheeks tensing. She placed the lifeless girl on the ground gently. Taking a deep breath, she relaxed her shoulder muscles, hoping the streak of anger would soon subside.

It didn't.

In a flash, she marched over to Eddie and stuck the barrel of her gun in his face.

He shrieked again, his eyes spouting tears. "Please! Don't! I didn't mean to! It was an accident! I take it back! I take it back!"

The metal dimpled his cheek.

"I don't give a shit!" Jill yelled through her teeth. "She was just a girl! Do you understand me? Just a girl! She was scared, goddammit! Scared and you fucking killed her!" Her finger teased the trigger. She closed her eyes.

Eddie begged.

She bit her bottom lip. Squeezed the trigger.

Not hard enough.

She let the gun fall against her hip.

Somewhere below, the alien beasts snarled. They were close. And they had located their quarry.

Jill pinched away tears from the corners of her eyes. "Come on. Get up. We're wasting time. We keep dicking around here and we'll all be dead."

She moved toward the stairwell.

CJ followed her, ignoring Eddie's reaching arms. Abandoned, Eddie began to sob again. Heavy, chest writhing sobs. Slowly, he picked himself off the ground and hustled after what remained of his group, jogging after them like a small child whose parents threatened to leave him behind because of an unnecessary tantrum.

From the ground, Brinks waved them goodbye and wished them luck.

Below, the monsters lurked. In a series of shrill vocalizations, they called for more bloodshed. Their footfalls were heard clearly as they moved in pursuit of more nourishment.

The hunt continued.

27.

By the time the three sharkoids exited the stairwell, Brinks had managed an upright sitting position, breathing heavily and reflecting back on his shitty, less-than-satisfying life. He examined each life choice in great detail, kicking himself for never trying new things, aspirations his drunk father told him he'd never be good at. The asshole had always told him he'd never amount to anything, a true waste of flesh and blood, an embarrassment that they shared the same DNA. One of the things Brinks regretted most was not slitting the old man's throat during one of his infamous, couch-bound comas. Another was not trying out for the school basketball team. He had always been shorter than most boys his age, but damn, he could shoot the three like Reggie Miller in his prime. He'd missed out on so much—prom, class trips, college, getting laid before he reached twenty-one without having to pay for it. All because of his asshole father and his non-existent mother. At least she had the good sense to see where the Brinks family was headed and killed herself before things took a drastic downward turn.

Or was her suicide the downward turn? He couldn't remember anymore and wasn't sure why the thought came to him now.

I guess that's just what you think about before you die.

He hated the fact that he was about to draw his last breath in this shit-splat hotel while his father, seventy-something now, was probably living the high life in some trailer park community, getting laid and blackout drunk each and every night. Banging the neighbors' wives. Enjoying whiskey-induced comas.

Fucking asshole.

Brinks watched the three sharkoids glide down the hallway in fluid fashion, as if they were coasting through the water. They reminded him of those dinosaurs in that Steven Spielberg adaptation, the ones that resembled giant turkeys. Birdlike. Fluid movement. Swift in pursuit. Manufactured to kill. Bred for violence, designed for malice.

Brinks recalled what happened to Evan down at the beach, and knew he was about to receive the same fate.

He gripped the knife at his side. If he was going out, he was taking at least one of the fuckers out with him. As they zipped down the hall, barreling at him with tremendous speed, he readied the knife into a slashing position. He'd admired their quickness, having never seen something on two legs move so fast before.

Fin-Head led the pack. Hammerhead and Mohawk towed closely. They spread apart in a V-pattern, typical pack-hunter mentality. The pattern was meant to confuse its prey, making it impossible to tell from which direction the first strike would come. The Goon Squad had used this strategy on several occasions. The target would expect the attack to come from the front, and while the target analyzed the situation and its defense, the main attack would come from the flank, hard and fast, without mercy. Unfortunately for the sharkoids, the hallway was too narrow to execute flawless subterfuge. Not that they needed it. *Their* target was weak and would offer little resistance.

Brinks knew he'd have to guess. He focused on Fin-Head, the clear alpha. He readied the blade.

And the attack came from the sides, just as he predicted.

And prepared for.

He turned to his left and stabbed upward, taking Hammerhead by surprise. The knife slipped into the black, rubbery flesh with the smoothness of a professional diver hitting calm waters at the perfect perpendicular trajectory. An ichorous soup sprayed from the opening, showering Brinks in the alien goo. He felt the liquid coat him, move over his flesh like an army of insects. He couldn't tell immediately, but the blood felt alive and on the move, seeking knew refuge. It crawled over him, pursuing other ways inside his body. He ignored the peculiar sensation of being enveloped in the alien sap and twisted the knife, inserting it deeper until the hilt was good and buried. Once the knife disappeared into the sharkoid's throat, he injected his hand, grasping for whatever he could hold on to and rip free. He felt the thing's spine and started yanking with all his strength, intending to excise it.

Then the pain settled in, explosions of anguish blooming on his shoulder and leg. The agony registered with his brain, which relayed the message to the rest of him that this was it, he was in a degree of trouble from which he would not survive. He glanced over his other shoulder and watched Fin-Head and Mohawk rip away pieces of his flesh and muscle with their jaws, maul him with their long-clawed fingers. Ribbons of blood flared in the air before him, droplets of incarnadine dancing in the air like Christmas pixies. Hanging onto Hammerhead's spine, he attempted to pull himself free, but the pain in his chest from the bullet wound limited his motion, brought him back down to reality and killed off his delusions of a hard-fought escape.

He lost his grip on Hammerhead and the sharkoid fell back, back knocking against the wall. It coughed, the black syrup sputtering over its lips, leaking across the floor. Before Fin-Head and Mohawk opened up Brinks's stomach and began choosing which parts to consume first, he watched Hammerhead's body fall limp.

Lifeless.

He had won. He'd killed the thing.

The sense of satisfaction was so overwhelming that the brutality of his own evisceration barely registered with his nerves.

His death was numb.

Painless.

The last remaining member of the Goon Squad was retired.

28.

Using his shoulder and left arm combined, Eddie popped open the hatch with relative ease. He clambered onto the roof with the gracefulness of a hippopotamus. After he was safely on, he spun back and assisted CJ over the riser, Jill pushing up on his bottom from below.

Once CJ was on the flat, tarpapered roof, he collapsed on his back and looked up at the never-ending sheet of slate that was now the sky. The sprawling, starless expanse spat on him, a prelude of the downpour to come.

Jill jumped over the roof hatch's threshold and immediately knelt beside the kid. "You okay?"

Ignoring her concern, he closed his eyes and squirmed in place, his body feeling like it had been set ablaze from the inside out. A hot pain spiked his bad knee, sending excruciating spasms down his calf. Jill placed her hand on his shoulder and tried to keep him from moving around, not wanting him to exhaust what remained of his energy.

"CJ?" she asked, rubbing his chest as if she were testing the softness of a new blanket.

"Damn it!" he shouted, clutching his knee.

"What happened?"

"My bad knee. Fuck, it hurts!"

"Can you walk?"

The thought of putting pressure on it made him grind his teeth. "No. I don't think so."

Jill nodded at Eddie. "Help me carry him over there." She pointed to the edge of the roof. A hip-high wall fenced in the entire area. "We'll lean him against the wall."

Eddie looked skyward. A bolt of lightning zagged across the dusky night, closely followed by a grumble of thunder. "We can't stay up here." His voice trembled.

Jill snapped her fingers at him. "Hey! Pay attention!"

Eddie craned his head toward her.

"Help me," she said.

Eddie ambled over as if stuck in a drug-induced daze.

Reluctantly, he helped her carry CJ's crippled body across the roof, sitting him up against the wall.

Once they were finished, Eddie paced back and forth, mumbling to himself.

"Buddy, you need to relax," Jill said sharply. "We'll be safe up here. Those things can't get to us."

"You don't know that, lady," Eddie snapped.

Jill opened her mouth to reply but closed it, realizing she, in fact, didn't *know* that, didn't know anything about the terrible creatures that were stalking them.

That was when they heard movement. At the base of the hatch. Footsteps, shuffling. Something growled, a predatory warning. Something clinked against the metal rungs. The three of them exchanged glances.

They found us, their expressions said.

Eddie was the only one to voice his dread. "Jesus Christ, they know where we are. They found us, they actually fucking found us!"

Jill fixed her gaze on the open hatch.

CJ swallowed the heartbeat in his throat. "Close the hatch," he whispered. "Close the fucking hatch."

Jill shushed him. She kept her finger over her mouth as she whispered, "They don't know we're up here. They can't possibly." Her leery-eyed glance found Eddie. "Unless..." She studied the sticky crimson art on the bartender's shirt.

"Unless what?" Eddie said, following her gaze. "Oh fuck. Oh Jesus fuck. No."

"Unless they can smell you," Jill said in a tone above a whisper.

To CJ, it made sense. If the things were truly part shark, then they could have adopted a keen sense of smell. It all depended on how their DNA was coded. Though they weren't aquatic creatures, CJ thought—judging from their anatomy—they'd do quite well in the water. On the other hand, CJ had seen what they were capable of as land-roaming bipeds, which made them quite unique.

Shark-like humans.

Perfect killing machines.

A whole new species.

Where did they come from?

He thought back to the rumors he had heard over the last decade while working for Big Tom. The fabled underwater research facility in the middle of the Gulf. He thought back to what he and Duke had found—hunks of metal, floating bodies, the gargantuan black shark.

What were they doing down there?

Experiments. Terrible things. An ungodly mess.

CJ tasted salt on his tongue. The rain washed away his tears but failed to cleanse his broken spirit.

* * *

"Oh fuck, I did this to us," Eddie said. He was spinning around in a short, circular pattern when Jill marched over to him and clapped her hand over his mouth.

"Shut the fuck up!" she whispered.

Over the patter of rain, they heard something heavy land on one of the metal rungs of the hatch's ladder. The sound rang out like a gong.

"Shit!" Jill yelled, immediately removing her hand from Eddie's lips. She scurried over to the hatch. Delicate with her stride because the tarpapered roof had become soaked and slippery, Jill kept her balance the whole way there. She reached the hatch in time to see one of the creatures, the one sporting a single crest on its head, rise up out of the hole.

"Motherfucker!" she screamed, slamming the metallic cover down on its skull. The creature released a noise that was part hiss, part bark, and heard with perfect clarity over the rainfall chatter. The monstrosity didn't lose its grip and plummet to the floor like Jill had envisioned. Instead, it heaved its body upward and popped the cover back. Jill drove it back down again, leading with her shoulder, this time putting her entire 140-pound frame into it.

"A little help here!" she called back to Eddie, but instead of looking for ways to help, the son of a bitch was seeking an alternate escape route, peering over the side of the hotel as if he were judging the distance, calculating the chances of surviving a fall that high. The idea was ridiculous; a plunge from that height would break every bone in his body, and if he was lucky, kill him instantly.

Eddie never came to her aid. He kept wandering around the outskirts of the roof, occasionally looking over the wall, occasionally grunting in frustration and ignoring the situation unfolding behind him.

Jill was suddenly thrown from the hatch with violent force. She tumbled across the roof and skidded to a stop. Looking back in horror, she watched Fin-Head emerge from the opening, gracefully springing out of the hatch like a frog across a pond full of water lilies.

Shit!

Out of the corner of her eye, Jill noticed Eddie clambering the wall. He was glancing over his shoulder, his eyes immediately drawn to the creature leaving the hatch. Fear fixed his face with deep furrows. His body trembled as he sobbed. Jill read the words that were coming out between his writhing lips.

"I'm sorry," he said. "God, I'm so sorry."

As Fin-Head darted toward him, Eddie turned and leapt. He disappeared into the dark of night, and if a blast of thunder hadn't sounded a moment later, Jill and CJ would have heard the crunch of Eddie's body splintering apart when it impacted the concrete patio.

Fin-Head had followed Eddie to the edge and scaled the wall. It leaned over the edge and examined the remains of its quarry, tracking the fall with narrowed, human eyes. After glimpsing the fractured frame, deeming the fresh meal lost, it rotated back to its other options.

Jill watched another sharkoid climb out of the hatch. Long ivory talons clinked on the metal, causing shivers to radiate down her spine. Mohawk pulled itself out of the mouth of the hatch and into view. Its teeth sparkled despite its maw being saturated in blood. Its skin glistened even under the dim moon, a shimmering black. To Jill, the atrocities looked like something fabricated on a Hollywood movie set. She was waiting for the moment they unzipped their costumes, revealing a pair of chuckling stuntmen, elated to have pulled off such an elaborate, convincing prank. She couldn't help but think this was all part of some twisted game, one designed by Neil Pickard, payback for the cold shoulder she'd given him over the last two years.

Impossible.

The creatures weren't fakes. Her eyes did not deceive. Call it "officer instinct" or whatever, but she knew these creatures were as tangible as the big black shark that snapped Pickard in half. In fact, the more she thought about it, the more the creatures held a similar resemblance. It was the black skin, she thought, pulled tight against their bone structure. The trio of sharkoids could have been its offspring.

Maybe that's exactly what they are.

Her taxed mind cranked out endless scenarios of how the next few minutes might play out, but each ended with her okay and safe and returning home to her bed and her boring life and her bad dates she arranged via bad dating websites.

The two creatures slinked ahead, holding their hands out as if they meant to grab hold of something. Their mouths stretched wide, displaying every single shard of tooth capable of shearing human flesh down to the bone. As they closed the gap between a crestfallen CJ, Jill removed the gun from her waistband, aimed it at Mohawk's head, and fired. The bullet connected with the side of its head, just missing the sweet spot between its eyes, her intended target. A mist of onyx fired up from the point of entry, mixing with the already-dark atmosphere. The black, pulpy grume landed on the tarpaper, blending with its backdrop. Jill lined her second shot when something moved in her peripherals.

"Um… Jill?" CJ asked, his voice shaky with distress. "We have a little situation here."

She was already on it. The black blood had collected itself in small puddles and began working its way across the roof like raindrops cascading down a windowpane.

That black shit is moving! Jill almost shouted, following the inky substance with her gun. It was alive, crawling toward CJ like a spreading pool of spilt milk. Seeing as the roof had zero pitch, Jill couldn't visualize how that was too possible. But then again, before today giant black sharks and human sharkoid creatures only lurked within bad dreams, not real life. So why not a traveling puddle of black mud?

She remembered the science lab and what Pickard had shown her the night before, the black substance they found infesting the cadaver's innards. The stuff that looked like microscopic black spiders. They were here. Living. Spreading. Looking for a new home to inhabit. Something warm and capable.

Something like CJ.

The two sharkoids grew closer, chasing after the obsidian splash. Mohawk ignored the leaking hole in the side of his head, stalking his prey as if nothing had happened. Jill rushed forward and grabbed CJ by his collar, yanking him out harm's way. The kid seemed to weigh a ton and she felt her muscles ignite as she pulled him along.

Fin-Head and Mohawk screeched, then sprinted forward with catlike quickness. Jill squeezed off two shots in rapid succession. One plugged Mohawk in the chest, the impact punching him sideways. The beast somehow managed to keep his feet, but the bullet temporarily ended his pursuit. Fin-Head caught a bullet in his neck. Onyx fluids burst from the entry wound, spilling down his chest like cola from the mouth of an aluminum can. The injury didn't seem to affect the creature as much as Jill would have guessed (or liked). However, Fin-Head only managed three steps before he dropped to his knees, wheezing, covering the bullet hole which spat dark clay through the cracks of his long, curved fingers.

Three bullets left, she counted silently.

"Can you move?" Jill asked CJ, keeping her eyes glued to the dangers lurking before her.

CJ grimaced with unbridled pain. "I think…"

She didn't hesitate; with the monsters reeling, she tucked her weapon back into her waistband, hooked her arms under CJ's shoulders and lifted him to his feet. His legs were like pudding, and she knew if she let go they'd be back to square one. Since she didn't feel like dragging him around the roof by his collar, she held onto him, letting him use her as a crutch, walking him over to the hip-high wall farthest from the recovering creatures. Once she had him situated, comfortable and leaning against the wall, she spun back and faced the fight.

"What are you going to do?" CJ asked, breathing heavily. The burst of spent energy had sucked all the air from his lungs.

"Three bullets left," she said, drawing her weapon. "I'm going to kill these fucks."

"Be careful."

Be careful, she thought. She knew what CJ meant: *Don't fucking miss.*

The two creatures renewed their violent fervor. Fin-Head stumbled, swaying back and forth like a late-night-early-morning drunk. Mohawk contorted its alien lips into a ferocious snarl, baring its white-stained-red teeth. Blood and obsidian ichor wept from its open maw. He readied his claws, those sharp killing tools, and strode ahead, fixing its gaze on the human that caused him to bleed. Jill could almost feel the monster's anger infiltrate her pores, filling her body with a cancerous sensation that traversed her circulatory system.

"Three bullets left," she repeated, adjusting her aim.

CJ watched, squinting against the torrents of rain and the sweeping shadows.

She moved forward, mapping her next move out in her mind. Fin-Head was as good as dead; she'd nicked something vital and the fucker was bound to bleed out soon. It was Mohawk who scared her. She had plugged the monster twice—*once in the fucking head*—and was still unable to put it down, even though her aim wasn't as true as she would have liked.

She had two options: use the last three bullets on Mohawk, ending him effectively and praying that Fin-Head bled out before he could do any further damage; or, put Fin-Head down immediately and get him out of the way. He was barely moving now and she was confident she could place the bullet right between his black, soulless eyes. That would leave her two bullets to pump into Mohawk. She could let the bastard get close, flirt with getting him into point-blank range. She could wait till the last possible second, press the nozzle to his shiny-onyx forehead and squeeze off the remaining shots, blowing his sickly gloppy brains all over the goddamn place.

She liked option two best.

As Mohawk picked up speed and closed the distance between

them, the heavens saturated the atmosphere with water, creating a misty veil in front of her.

Great, she thought, *another obstacle.*

The rain coupled with the black of night wouldn't help her aim, but her confidence evened the score. Her male co-workers often complimented her accuracy whenever they went to the range. *A goddamn natural,* they boasted.

Pride warmed over her. She aimed at Fin-Head, imagining a tiny red dot in the center of his slimy forehead. She squeezed the trigger and the first bullet left its home with a loud pop. The creature's brains ruptured from the fresh crater in his skull, an ebony burst of blood and brains. As Fin-Head stumbled forward in death, glimmering sable fluids sluiced from the hollow opening between his lifeless eyes. He fell forward, onto his face with a mild splash. A spreading black pool crept out from beneath his fallen frame and merged with the other alien party.

Jill eyed the animated lake of endless black. She hadn't forgotten about it, but Mohawk loomed near and he was now the top priority. The savage creature hunched down, preparing to launch himself at his quarry, his next meal. Jill turned the gun on the sharkoid, hoping not to need the second (and last) bullet.

The heavens opened and dumped buckets on them. As the clouds swirled and the atmosphere fogged with humidity, something odd happened, something Jill hadn't seen coming. Mohawk abandoned his hunched position and began to back away from Jill altogether. The creature looked around frantically, as if he'd caught the scent of a larger predator, unknowingly stumbled into its territory and suddenly realized his fatal error. Jill watched Mohawk swivel his head in all directions, peering into the darkness with such trepidation that she thought he looked suddenly human. She recognized something in his face, something she had witnessed plenty of tonight—fear.

The goddamn thing is afraid, she thought, smiling unknowingly.

Of what exactly filled her with chills.

Steam rose off its flesh, coiling wisps of thick fog. As this unfolded, Jill stepped forward, training the gun, focusing in on that sweet kill spot near the temple.

Then came the scream.

It was so loud Jill almost dropped the gun. The shrill, ear-splitting vocalization cut through the night, temporarily silencing the storm. Had there been anyone left on the island, perhaps vacationing at Sharkwater Beach, they would have heard the alien creature's outburst with almost perfect clarity. It sounded childlike. The screech sliced through Jill in more ways than one. It hit her emotionally while combing her eardrums, feeling like someone dragged a garden rake across the side of her brain.

She felt bad for the thing, whatever was happening to it.

Is this a tactic? she pondered. *Can it sense I'm about to blow its fucking brains out? Is it playing me?*

Then she recalled all the blood the trio of monsters had spilled. The smorgasbord of appendages haphazardly strewn throughout the bar. The ocean of gore that soaked into the hardwood floors, forever tainting its color and antique appearance. She remembered all of it and in that moment, she realized she shouldn't feel anything for the creature except hatred, scorn for its vicious nature. She knew the creature was only acting on primal instincts, but that didn't mean she should pity it.

No, it needed to die.

And Jill would make it so.

Not only was Mohawk caterwauling, but so was the migrant puddle of black blood. At first Jill thought it was her imagination, her ears tricking her mind into believing something so preposterous. Or maybe she thought it was the way the roof's acoustics interacted with Mohawk's pitch, making it sound like the noise was coming from all directions. But after about thirty seconds of the discordant whine, she knew the onyx pool was mimicking Mohawk's cry. Black foam bubbled on the surface of the sleek liquid, as if there were flames flickering beneath it, bringing the ungodly stew to a boil. Smoke curled up from the puddle, undulating in the air like the sudden disappearance of ghostly remains. The air became tainted, smelling like a chemical fire, acrid and eye-watering. It caused her stomach to somersault. There was also the faint odor of singed flesh which increased her nausea.

But the real issue was the noise. It had become so unbearable that she needed to end it. She aimed, visualizing an X on the creature's forehead. She closed her right eye and held her breath. Before pulling the trigger, she watched black fluids drip down Mohawk's face. It funneled off his arms, running like cheap makeup. She couldn't tell if the darkness and the downpour were deceiving her eyes, throwing illusions before her, but the alien sharkoid looked as if he were melting, which would explain the caterwauling. The pungent stench filling up the atmosphere suggested that what she was witnessing was real.

No illusions.

The thing is melting.

Now was her chance to eradicate the new species before it ever had a chance to join their ecosystem.

But she pulled the trigger at the wrong time. Mohawk dodged simultaneously with the shot. The bullet sailed past his head, disappearing immediately in the dark backdrop. Mohawk, his flesh still steaming, his eyes open and burning with sick rage, charged forth, fixing his gaze on Jill and the gun shaking between her hands.

She knew she didn't have much time; the creature closed the gap between them with unbelievable momentum. She aimed and fired her final shot, which pierced Mohawk's shoulder, spraying flowers of obsidian into the air.

Not a kill shot. Not even close.

She cursed and threw her empty weapon at the hostile being. It bounced off its slick, liquid flesh, the impact having about as much response as the last bullet—not much. Jill panicked. The beast narrowed the distance quickly. He was pissed off and Jill was public enemy number one. The thing would tear her apart savagely, within seconds if she chose not to struggle. Those barbed talons would flay her flesh with ease. Her bones were brittle compared to the sharkoid's strength—it could easily punch through her chest wall and remove her still-beating heart. She imagined Mohawk hoisting her innards over his head like the prestigious prizes in the center of a pinata.

The black blood continued to froth and boil, the rain wreaking havoc over it, reducing it to a stagnant pool of dark nothingness.

Jill turned and bolted for the edge of the roof. CJ had brought himself to a kneeling position on top of the wall. He called to her, reaching for her hand. She didn't know what plan he had in mind, but whatever it was was surely better than anything she had going. *Lure the bastard to the edge,* her inner voice urged. *Lure him to the edge and at the last second, when the beast is on you, jump aside and let him fall the way of Eddie Rudders.*

The long drop of death.

It wasn't a bad idea. Hell, it was her *only* idea.

It'll work, she told herself.

It had to, or she and CJ would be spending the rest of the evening being torn to gobbets.

In one motion, Jill jumped onto the wall, balanced herself, then spun around. She faced Mohawk who had reached the top speed of his hundred-meter dash, engaging long, galloping strides. Some of his black flesh had given way to raw, bleeding muscle. White pus and pink tissue showed through the scattered patchwork of rubbery skin.

The rain is melting its skin!

A bad chemical reaction to Earth's atmosphere would explain the sulfuric smell that nearly choked her. The creature's flesh deteriorated the same way acid would eat away corrosive articles. Whatever adaptive preparations the sharkoids' bodies had taken prior to coming ashore wasn't enough. It had yet to evolve, acclimate to the intricacies of an alien world.

Mohawk screeched his final battle cry. The last vocalization was filled with contempt and fear, a hint of agony. Mostly contempt for this planet's superior species. He and the others had desired to sit atop Earth's food chain, peer down on all they had conquered and scream a very different scream, one filled with an overwhelming sense of accomplishment.

Hustling toward his prey, Mohawk snarled, snapping his jaws, preparing to fill his gorge with flesh and muscle and blood and—

Jill felt something bounce into her hip, and she was flung aside. Her chest landed on top of the wall and she immediately rolled over, her back falling, crashing down on the roof. The four-foot drop punched the wind from her lungs but she paid no attention to the tightness in her chest and back. Instead, she glanced up and saw what had knocked her down with such force.

Who had knocked her down.

CJ crouched on the ledge, hands out in front of him the same way he would brace for a football block.

"No!" Jill screamed.

She cried out in protest, but it was too late. Mohawk had already hurled his massive body into her savior, shark tail whipping back and forth, barely visible against the shroud of night.

* * *

In that moment he thought of Duke, his mind frequently wandering toward the memories of his fallen friend. As Mohawk barreled toward Jill, he couldn't think of anything else. He kept seeing his goofy pal sink beneath the surface, never to return topside again. He also thought of how Duke's death was all his fault. It was CJ who planted the seed to forget the job search and become entrepreneurs. It was he who had convinced him to pour his life savings into buying their own boat. It was he who had suggested they stay out and fish late that day in order to build up a respectable inventory. It was because of him they were out there in the first place. CJ decided he shouldn't be the one to live; he should have gone down with the ship, met the mouth of the monster just like his best friend.

It all felt so unfair.

In the brief moment the creature darted toward Jill, he decided she should be the one to live. Why shouldn't she? If it weren't for her, they would have been slaughtered downstairs along with the rest of the fishermen. She had kept her wits about her and guided them to safety. Plus, after Eddie killed that frightened college girl, she had kept calm and refused to let her emotions get the best of her. She could have easily ended his life right then and there. But no. She let him live. Not only that, but she helped him to safety. Guided him to the roof. Even tried to talk him out of his leap of faith. So, yes. She deserved to live.

And he did not. He was a failure. He'd let down his best friend, the one person in the world that had counted on him.

He summoned the remaining strength from his waist down,

swiveled his hips, and pushed himself forward. Throwing his arms out, he made sure to direct Jill's body in a way that she could not fall *off* the roof, but rather, back onto the tarpaper. His plan worked and he watched the woman tumble down, safely landing where he intended. He had pushed her with force because he wanted to make sure she didn't land awkwardly in the opposite direction.

She flipped over and looked directly up at him, her eyes wide with surprise.

He winked at her the second before the monster bowled into him, wiping him clean off his feet. He held onto Mohawk's slippery wet skin, a task that proved almost too difficult. He lost his grasp, but it didn't matter; the two of them were already over the edge, plummeting through the dark. A hard, sandy demise awaited them. The ground approached much slower than he expected. But it didn't matter. CJ always wanted to feel what it was like to fly.

And he fell. And fell. In his ear the creature screamed, an alien shriek that needled the epicenter of his brain. He tuned it out, listened to the rush of air all around him.

He closed his eyes and became one with the black.

He barely felt his neck break.

THE AFTERMATH

She didn't know at what point she passed out. Sometime after the last remaining monster met gravity and lost, sometime before sunrise.

She was alone.

That comfortable solitude.

When she opened her eyes it was morning. The sun beat down on her face and warmed her flesh. Not a gray cloud hung in the sky, just an ever-stretching blanket of seaside blue. She shielded her aching eyes and glanced around. Pushing herself to her feet, she spotted the hatch, still open, inviting her inside. She had no intentions of going back down there. There was nothing but the smell of bloody violence wafting up from below, and her stomach frothed just thinking about the aftermath of the carnage.

On the tarpaper, the black lake of blood—once a living, traveling colony of microscopic spiders—now lay still, depleted of life and crusted, a transparent film coating it like dried countertop grease. She rubbed her toe in it, and the sludge moved like the thickest slop of river mud. Disgusted, she screwed her lips up and moved on. She toured the top of the roof, her stomach aching, clamoring for nutrition.

Key Water Island was eerily silent. A shift in a wind. That was it. The fragrance of saltwater climbed up her nose and she thought it was the most refreshing scent in all the world. She breathed in deeply, coating her lungs with the sensory sweetness, good as a bouquet of fresh roses.

Noise. In the distance.

She craned her head eastward.

A small dot.

Pickard's chopper. He had actually called it in. She had thought he flaked on his promise, like he had on so many others. But, no. In the end, he had followed through.

Son of a bitch.

She was rescued.

* * *

The chopper touched down on the roof and she ran to it like a long-lost lover. Over the obnoxious noise of the propeller, the man sitting in the passenger seat cupped his hands over his mouth and shouted, "Jill?" as he hopped out. He wore gold-rimmed aviators with black-out glass and a stretched brown suit, giving him that cool-to-be-hip scholarly appearance. His shaggy hair kicked around in the whirlwind the chopper's blade provided. She knew the type. The kind of professor who sat around the campfire, smoking reefer with his students, reading from Henry David Thoreau or Ayn Rand, roasting fucking marshmallows and dropping mescaline.

"Yes," she replied, sounding breathless.

"Neil sent me."

"Perfect." She rushed over to him. She detected the scent of marijuana from a good distance away.

"Where is that dude?" Professor Pot-Breath asked.

She swallowed. "He didn't... he isn't... It's a long story."

"Jesus, are you okay?" he asked, nodding at the dark rusty stains on her clothing.

She glanced down. "Oh, yeah. Not my blood."

Before he could ask whose blood it was, his gaze wandered and eventually settled on something behind her. She turned as he lowered his glasses to rest on the edge of his nose.

Fin-Head's corpse lay in a pool of crusty black blood which looked like a lumpy pile of tar from their distance.

"What the fuck is that thing?" he asked, oddly amused.

"Like I said—long story."

"I'll say."

Jill thought he was so high he probably thought this whole thing was a joke. She didn't press the matter.

He nodded back, out to sea. "Have anything to do with why they're here?"

Jill followed his gesture. In the distance, dozens of specks populated the horizon. They looked like gnats buzzing about. Sounded like them, too. As they grew bigger, the sounds of their approach grew louder. Soon, she discovered they weren't insects at all.

More helicopters.

Big black ones. Government? Had to be. Who else would come out into the Gulf this far?

"Let's get out of here," Jill demanded.

"I second that," Pot-Breath said, helping her inside.

Within a minute, they were a hundred feet over the island and still climbing. Soon, the entire island shrank into view. She spotted what appeared to be a beached whale on the west end, but after a few seconds her brain allowed her to piece the magnificent beast together: the giant black shark. Its stomach had been torn open, leaving gulls and other seabirds to feast upon its rancid meat. They swooped and swarmed the carcass, each taking with them a meaty souvenir.

Jill turned her head.

"Look! A whale!" Pot-Breath shouted with the interest of a schoolboy in an aquarium full of deadly sharks.

Jill didn't have the energy to explain everything. She sat in silence and retrieved her phone from her pocket. Two percent. More battery than she would have guessed. She thumbed through her e-mails, sifting through the junk, the click-bait bullshit. She found one message that read, "You have a new match!" She opened it and checked out the guy's profile pic. Andy Erma had horned-rimmed glasses and a gap between his front teeth she could fit her fist through. His hobbies included Minecraft and collecting old-school coloring books.

She rolled her eyes and powered off her phone, slipped it back into her pocket, and pulled herself into a ball, tucking her knees against her chest and wrapping her forearms around them. The pose comforted her in a way she could not explain.

The crew of helicopters rushed past her, twelve in all. She followed them with burning curiosity, though deep down she knew why they were here.

In a matter of minutes, her suspicions were confirmed.

The island erupted with rolling balls of fire. The choppers circled the island, pummeling the sand and jungle with nuclear explosives, bathing the tropical expanse with mushroom clouds and hellfire. Soon, all that remained of Sharkwater Beach was smoke and flames, cleansing the world of all the dirty things that had happened there.

Jill closed her eyes and dreamed of sleep.

* * *

It fought off the gulls and scavenger birds that picked its mother apart. It bit back. The gulls screeched. Some of it was ingested and began working hard to overtake the bird's central nervous system. It didn't take long. Soon, it was in complete control.

Then came bigger birds. They posed a threat. The collective alien substance sensed danger.

It was time to leave.

The infected bird flew upward but was burnt black by a roiling cloud of fire.

The rest of black matter crawled out of its mother and slithered across the sand, leaving the gulls to feast upon the flesh of its carrier. It escaped toward the water. The remaining island life was obliterated by the anvils of death.

The black puddle reached the shoreline and allowed itself to become swallowed by the waves. The big teal drink welcomed the black fluid, absorbed it, and became one.

Collectively, the alien species decided to return to its hiding place before the humans had discovered it.

It returned to the deep, where it rested for another ten million years.

THE END.

Tim Meyer dwells in a dark cave near the Jersey Shore. He's an author, husband, father, podcast host, blogger, coffee connoisseur, beer enthusiast, and explorer of worlds. He writes horror, mysteries, science fiction, and thrillers, although he prefers to blur genres and let the stories fall where they may.

You can follow Tim at https://timmeyerwrites.com
OR like his Facebook page here:
www.facebook.com/authortimmeyer

SEVEREDPRESS

CHECK OUT OTHER GREAT DEEP SEA THRILLERS

THEY RISE
by Hunter Shea

Some call them ghost sharks, the oldest and strangest looking creatures in the sea.

Marine biologist Brad Whitley has studied chimaera fish all his life. He thought he knew everything about them. He was wrong. Warming ocean temperatures free legions of prehistoric chimaera fish from their methane ice suspended animation. Now, in a corner of the Bermuda Triangle, the ocean waters run red. The 400 million year old massive killing machines know no mercy, destroying everything in their path. It will take Whitley, his climatologist ex-wife and the entire US Navy to stop them in the bloodiest battle ever seen on the high seas.

SERPENTINE
by Barry Napier

Clarkton Lake is a picturesque vacation spot located in rural Virginia, great for fishing, skiing, and wasting summer days away.

But this summer, something is different. When butchered bodies are discovered in the water and along the muddy banks of Clarkton Lake, what starts out as a typical summer on the lake quickly turns into a nightmare.

This summer, something new lives in the lake...something that was born in the darkest depths of the ocean and accidentally brought to these typically peaceful waters.

It's getting bigger, it's getting smarter...and it's always hungry.

CHECK OUT OTHER GREAT
DEEP SEA THRILLERS

MEGA
by Jake Bible

There is something in the deep. Something large. Something hungry. Something prehistoric.

And Team Grendel must find it, fight it, and kill it.

Kinsey Thorne, the first female US Navy SEAL candidate has hit rock bottom. Having washed out of the Navy, she turned to every drink and drug she could get her hands on. Until her father and cousins, all ex-Navy SEALS themselves, offer her a way back into the life: as part of a private, elite combat Team being put together to find and hunt down an impossible monster in the Indian Ocean. Kinsey has a second chance, but can she live through it?

THE BLACK
by Paul E Cooley

Under 30,000 feet of water, the exploration rig Leaguer has discovered an oil field larger than Saudi Arabia, with oil so sweet and pure, nations would go to war for the rights to it. But as the team starts drilling exploration well after exploration well in their race to claim the sweet crude, a deep rumbling beneath the ocean floor shakes them all to their core. Something has been living in the oil and it's about to give birth to the greatest threat humanity has ever seen.

"The Black" is a techno/horror-thriller that puts the horror and action of movies such as Leviathan and The Thing right into readers' hands. Ocean exploration will never be the same."

CHECK OUT OTHER GREAT DEEP SEA THRILLERS

HELL'S TEETH
by Paul Mannering

In the cold South Pacific waters off the coast of New Zealand, a team of divers and scientists are preparing for three days in a specially designed habitat 1300 feet below the surface.

In this alien and savage world, the mysterious great white sharks gather to hunt and to breed.

When the dive team's only link to the surface is destroyed, they find themselves in a desperate battle for survival. With the air running out, and no hope of rescue, they must use their wits to survive against sharks, each other, and a terrifying nightmare of legend.

MONSTERS IN OUR WAKE
by J.H. Moncrieff

In the idyllic waters of the South Pacific lurks a dangerous and insatiable predator; a monster whose bloodlust and greed threatens the very survival of our planet...the oil industry. Thousands of miles from the nearest human settlement, deep on the ocean floor, ancient creatures have lived peacefully for millennia. But when an oil drill bursts through their lair, Nøkken attacks, damaging the drilling ship's engine and trapping the desperate crew. The longer the humans remain in Nøkken's territory, struggling to repair their ailing ship, the more confrontations occur between the two species. When the death toll rises, the crew turns on each other, and marine geologist Flora Duchovney realizes the scariest monsters aren't below the surface.

Made in the USA
Las Vegas, NV
29 May 2021